'You marrie **muttered.**

Kathleen flinched, the truth. But she had to keep up the pretence. She raised her eyes to Lorcan. 'Don't condemn me. You don't know the circumstances—'

'And now he's dead.' Lorcan continued. 'Ballykisteen is yours when I thought it was mine. Astonishing luck on your part—or was it judgement? My congratulations.'

'No. Harry left the estate to me and you, to be shared equally.'

Lorcan sat back in his chair. 'Then you've got something I want. And I mean to have it.'

Childhood in Portsmouth meant grubby knees, flying pigtails and happiness for **Sara Wood**. Poverty drove her from typist and seaside landlady to teacher, till writing finally gave her the freedom her Romany blood craved. Happily married, she has two handsome sons: Richard is calm, dependable, drives tankers; Simon is a roamer—silversmith, roofer, welder—always with beautiful girls. Sara lives in the Cornish countryside. Her glamorous writing life alternates with her passion for gardening which allows her to be carefree and grubby again!

Recent titles by the same author:

THE IMPATIENT GROOM
A HUSBAND'S VENDETTA

THE INNOCENT MISTRESS

BY
SARA WOOD

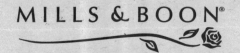
MILLS & BOON®

First published in Great Britain 1999
Harlequin Mills & Boon Limited,
Eton House, 18-24 Paradise Road, Richmond, Surrey TW9 1SR

© Sara Wood 1999

ISBN 0 263 81931 0

Set in Times Roman 10½ on 11½ pt.
01-0002-52237 C1

Printed and bound in Spain
by Litografia Rosés, S.A., Barcelona

CHAPTER ONE

KATHLEEN thought of Lorcan and shivered. It was as though a sword had been hanging on a thread above her head for the past three months; the thread was slowly getting weaker and one day soon down it would come. That would be the day Lorcan phoned.

Nervously she imagined their first meeting, vividly picturing his inevitable contempt and his brutal indifference to the lives he'd disrupt. There wasn't a thing she could do to stop him. He had a legal right to ruin her life, she thought, biting down hard on her lower lip.

Her apprehension had begun soon after Harry's death, when the solicitor had put a weekly advert in the *Irish Times* asking for any information on the whereabouts of Harry's brother Lorcan. From then on each morning she woke she feared that it might be the last she'd spend at the beautiful Georgian manor house.

If Lorcan should come back to claim his inheritance nothing would ever be the same again. She and her baby would be homeless; it was as simple as that.

'Are you deeply attached to that runner bean, Kathleen, me darlin', or can it join its little friends in the basket?'

She blinked, the nightmare scenario disturbed by Declan's lazy teasing. To her surprise, she saw that the grubby tips of her fingers were just visible from beneath the long sleeves of her enormous sweater and were twisting and turning the bean like a worry bead.

'Idiot!'

With deadly accuracy she flicked the bean at him, rolled back the trailing sleeves and continued picking, stacking

5

the long, crisp pods into a box bearing the inscription 'Ballykisteen Manor. Organic Produce'.

'I was wondering,' she went on, as dignified as anyone just scraping five foot could be, 'how we'd cope if Lorcan *did* get in touch.'

'Sure, it's not worth bothering your ugly little head about,' Declan said with the affectionate rudeness of a life-long friend. 'There's been no response to the advert and it's been withdrawn. End of story. He's had his chance and missed it.'

Superstitiously, she tried not to raise her hopes too much, just in case.

'Maybe. But I'm not relaxing yet.'

'Well, I am. Ballykisteen is yours.'

'Half of it,' she corrected glumly, shooing away a clutch of glint-eyed and hopeful hens from the pile of bright green beans.

'And isn't that amazing?! I still can't think what Harry was doing, sharing it between the two of you! I know he wasn't himself those last few weeks, but surely he can't have been *that* confused?' Declan sounded outraged on her behalf. 'He loathed Lorcan like poison!'

She sighed, shutting her mind to the dreadful memories of the past year. 'Poor Harry! I suppose he wanted to inflict his debts on his brother as a final gesture of hatred.'

'Maybe! But those debts are yours by rights and I'll thump anyone who says otherwise!' Declan declared, bringing a wry smile to her pensive face as he'd intended. 'Come on, you know I'm right. You were Harry's wife, for pity's sake!'

Kathleen winced, and kept silent. No one knew that she and Harry had never married. She'd always felt guilty about the deception they'd practised on everyone but had sworn an oath never to breathe a word of it.

However, if Lorcan appeared at the Manor one day, if he ever knew the truth…

Her face paled beneath its healthy outdoor glow. It didn't bear thinking about. She was scared for her baby's future. Heaven help them both, she thought nervously, if the stony-hearted Lorcan discovered her secret!

Barely two miles to go before he was home! Lorcan let out a whoop of triumph as a sudden energy poured into his screaming muscles and every corner of his weary body.

Fired by the adrenaline—and with more gusto than accuracy—he burst into song, accompanying one of the Irish folk tunes on his car radio that had kept him awake since shortly after dawn.

Or, according to his body clock, it had been midnight. He did a quick calculation. That meant if it was breakfast-time in Boston now…it must be almost lunchtime here. No wonder his digestive system didn't know where it was!

He snatched a quick bite of the beef sandwich he'd grabbed in Galway and wished fervently it was hash browns and eggs easy-over. So did his stomach. Knots of discomfort had taken up residence there.

It couldn't be nerves, that was for sure. His were armour-plated.

Thoughtfully he massaged his tense midriff with a tightly clenched fist. Eight years he'd been away, he marvelled. And if Harry hadn't died prematurely, he'd never have returned at all.

As a point of honour, he searched for the merest hint of sadness but found none. He grunted, a brief sourness marring his joy. Why *should* he mourn Harry? His brother's lies had branded him with so many sins in the book that his reputation had been shredded like tickertape.

Lorcan's teeth tore viciously at the sandwich. The FitzGeralds had adopted them from different families;

Harry from birth, he eleven years later at the age of nine. It had been a fatal mistake. Instead of being companions for one another they'd become instant enemies: the invader and the invaded.

He had to admit that in those days he'd been even less charming than Heathcliff with a hangover. But at their first meeting there had been no need for the stocky Harry to suggest a game of Vikings—where the swords had been garden spades. Harry's first blow had split Lorcan's face open.

Now there was no Harry to give him hell. He fingered the faint scar carving an unerring path down his strong cheekbone, which had given countless women a perfect opening gambit.

Women… His eyes changed from bright sea-green to cold malachite in seconds as he thought of one woman in particular. There would be no Kathleen, either. What an ambitious and scheming little tramp she'd been!

Born illegitimate to his father's housekeeper, she'd seemed a fragile waif as a child: gypsy-dark, with National Health spectacles, spots and train-track braces, all of which had made her the easy victim of persistent bullying.

Yet by her mid-teens she'd turned into a cracker, every curvaceous inch miraculously perfect. The braces had gone to reveal even white teeth in an ever-laughing mouth, her sight had been corrected and her skin…

His fingers tightened on the steering wheel. Touching her had been like stroking living silk.

Impatiently he corrected an over-steer before he careered into a wild fuchsia hedge. That was the trouble with Kathleen, he reflected grimly; she tempted you into lush, exotic danger.

Wicked, feckless and deeply flawed, she'd been a greedy little minx. Sex-mad, power-mad. At seventeen she'd kissed him senseless and left him reeling. An hour later she'd been giggling in bed with Harry. The next morning he'd seen her in a clinch with Declan, the gardener's son!

He grunted. Some operator! It had taken a lobotomy on his emotions to forget her.

He muttered an irritated exclamation and adjusted his position. Despite his supposed exhaustion, one part of his anatomy seemed to have leapt into life.

Balefully he flexed his near-rigid fingers and steel girder spine in an attempt to divert his sexual ache. Lusting after her was a waste of precious energy. He'd sooner eat raw sirloin steak in a cage of ravenous tigers.

Gradually he regained control of his treacherous testosterone. But his pulses continued to drum through his body, a sure sign that sweet Kate had left an unresolved legacy of anger and resentment there.

It was just as well that she and her mother had long gone from Ballykisteen, otherwise he would have been tempted to sideline his plans for the house—and concentrate his mind on devising a well-justified revenge.

His eyes glittered. Now that would really be something to look forward to in the future!

Kathleen flung the last few beans into the basket and adjusted the belt holding up her one-size-too-big jeans. She heard a snoring coming from the direction of her feet and the solemn line of her mouth curved into a fleeting smile. Her two mongrels lay lovingly across her work boots, the mange and maltreatment that had once plagued the dogs now a blessedly fading memory.

Bending down to fondle their soft ears, she shuddered to think what would happen to all her rescued animals if Lorcan muscled in and forced her to leave.

Nearby, on the path that ran through the walled vegetable garden, assorted cats with a variety of disabilities were contentedly sunning themselves. In the meadow beyond she could hear the geese complaining as the old donkey and two rescued Connemara ponies thundered up and down the neighbouring paddock in joyful play.

'I know this is rotten of me to say so,' she admitted, owning up to her sins, 'but I can't help hoping that Lorcan never shows his face here.'

'It would be a disaster, no word of a lie!' agreed Declan in tones of doom.

She straightened, caught unawares by a sudden prickling of hot tears. 'What do you think he'd do? Insist on buying me out?'

'You couldn't buy *his* share, that's for sure,' mused Declan.

'It's ridiculous. I can only lay my hands on a packet of money if the Manor is sold!' she complained. 'There's no doubt that I'd be forced to go. What will happen to Con and me, you, Bridget, the kids, Kevin, our customers…everyone who depends on our business?' Her voice began to shake with emotion.

'Don't get upset, darlin' girl—'

'I can't help it!' she cried in frustration. 'I've tried to be sensible and accept the situation, but I've thought about it, night after night since Harry's death, and I'm sick with worry!'

Declan shot a look at her but she'd buried her head in the bean foliage to hide her distress. Tactfully he moved on to lift a few leeks.

'You'd *have* to share with him, then. Split the garden down the middle. Onions to the right, cabbages to the left,' he suggested with too-hearty cheerfulness. 'Take half the donkey each—insist on the eating end, mind. Tell him he's welcome to the goats and divide the house so that you get the kitchen and telly. How's that?'

Emerging from the foliage with scarlet flowers dotted about her thick curls, Kathleen grimaced, unable to muster up a smile even to be polite. Declan was a 'pleaser' who avoided conflict. He'd always go for the easy option.

But she and Lorcan could surely never live within ten miles of one another, let alone in the same building. His blistering scorn had left wounds she was still licking. In one vicious outburst he'd had her evicted and catapulted into a nightmare.

'Unworkable.' She screwed a lock of gleaming black hair in her fingers, her dark eyes awash with grim memories. 'Can you imagine the rows? They'd start earthquakes. He'd want to kick me into the gutter where he thinks I belong.' She sighed heavily. 'I just hope he never comes!'

'He won't. Stop worrying.'

But she couldn't. Lines of anxiety deepened between her winging brows. Lorcan had always frightened and fascinated her because he was unconventional. An unpredictable maverick. Harry had told her some very scary stories about him.

She'd been six when Lorcan had first arrived. That same day, his volcanic temper had erupted dramatically. For the rest of her life she would remember finding Harry whimpering like a baby, complaining that Lorcan had punched him without provocation.

Several hours had passed before Lorcan had been tracked down halfway along the old bog road, his shirt bloodstained from a wound on his face, which Harry had sworn was self-inflicted. From that moment on, all the children had been in awe of him.

Yet, she mused, her life had improved because of Lorcan. To her astonishment he'd taken it on himself to defend her from the kids at school. True to form, Declan hadn't stood up to the bullies at all.

It had been Lorcan who'd done that, Lorcan who'd comforted her when he'd found her in floods of tears during the school break one particular afternoon.

With gentle persistence he'd discovered there'd been a spiteful rumour that her hair was infested with nits. She'd been terrified it would be shaved off. People still remembered how he'd stormed into the classroom at the small village school, ignoring the teacher and letting rip with a scorching tirade which had left everyone shaking. The teacher included.

She snapped a crisp pod and chewed on it, puzzling over his contradictory behaviour. He'd been very sweet, almost tender in his concern, and as fierce as an avenging angel in his determination to crush the bullying.

Yet she had to admit that his behaviour had been in marked contrast to the terrible reputation he'd acquired as a pathological liar and rebel, with a temper on him like a wounded animal.

Even so, she conceded, he'd never hurt her in any way. Consequently his eventual cruelty to her had been a total shock. She went cold to the marrow to think of it. He had no mercy for his enemies.

And they were enemies now. She knew she had no honourable claim on the Manor that she adored—and that Lorcan might prise that fact out of her by fixing her with that terrible stare of his till she gabbled out the truth. And then she'd be told to pack her bags. She began to tremble from head to foot.

'Grand day,' commented Declan, unsuspecting.

Perfect. Wonderful house, blue sky, clouds clawing at the mountains, the sound of curlews piping… She looked around with increasing distress, picturing herself seeing all this for the last time…

No! She couldn't bear it! Her breath rasped painfully in her throat.

'I don't ever want to leave!' she blurted out, with such passion that she dislodged the slumbering dogs. 'I'd do anything to stay! I'd crawl. Beg him on bended knees to go away and leave us alone—'

'No, you wouldn't!' protested Declan, aghast.

Her eyes had grown huge and dark with panic. 'I would!' she cried brokenly. And to her amazement she realised that perhaps Ballykisteen *with* Lorcan might be preferable to not living at the Manor at all. 'If it comes to the crunch and he insists I go,' she said, her eyes dark with worry, 'I might plead to be his daily help, wash his dishes—perhaps even lick his wretched boots if he insisted!'

Declan grimly stuck his fork in the soil and strode over, clamping muddy hands the size of dinner plates on her bird-like shoulders. He looked deeply into her eyes and she felt immediately protected by this giant of a man, whose hair was as black and as wayward as hers.

'Boot polish leaves a nasty aftertaste in the mouth,' he warned.

'Oh, Dec!' she moaned, beyond all jokes. 'Don't let it happen to me!'

'It won't,' he soothed.

Her hands didn't quite meet around his broad back, but she squeezed him hard in desperation nevertheless. Awkwardly he stroked her hair. She wanted to believe him, but Dec would never stand up to Lorcan if it came to the crunch. She had a terrible sense of foreboding. The last time she'd been thrown out of Ballykisteen had been bad enough.

Crushed against Declan's massive chest, she felt her heavy silver locket pressing hard into her breastbone. And she thought of her first child, whose photograph lay within that locket; the son she'd loved and lost so many years ago.

She felt the pain slash through her body with the sharpness of a carving knife and despaired that she'd never been able to get over little Kieran's death. It had intensified her love for baby Conor, who was the most precious thing in the world to her now.

Because of Con, she'd sacrifice even her pride if it meant he'd be safe and protected. They *must* stay.

She drew in a shaky breath. She'd fight tooth and nail, wheedle, manipulate…do *anything*, to save Conor's birth-right.

Dooley's came into sight, the pub now painted a virulent pink and purple with turquoise fancywork around the doors and windows. As his eyes recovered from this and he entered the village, Lorcan's muscles loosened miraculously.

A long lazy bath and a hearty Irish meal with a pint of the black stuff—now that would set him up well!

And then… His eyes danced, a startling aquamarine in the gold of his face. He had such plans for the Manor! They'd make his mother's hair curl—and only the strongest of perms had ever done that before, he thought fondly.

Amused, he pictured his mother's surprise when he turned up. She'd suddenly stopped replying to his letters five years ago and Harry's curt note had made it clear that she blamed him for his adoptive father's death.

At that time he'd been so riven with guilt that he'd been unable to face the possibility of being rejected by her. A whole bunch of people had done so in his past. Rejection was something he couldn't handle and so he'd blanked his conscious mind to his mother's apparent desertion and spent every waking hour at work, the years speeding by like water running through his fingers.

Now Harry was dead, Lorcan felt confident that he could win her round. He chuckled, musing that he hadn't swotted endlessly in law school for nothing!

Through the open window he inhaled the evocative smell of clean, salt air. And with it came the unmistakable aroma of burning turf, the slabs of dried peat which were used as fuel in the hearths of Ballykisteen's traditional longhouses. He was pleased to see that some of the buildings were still thatched here, the roofs netted with rope to keep them secure during the violent Atlantic gales.

Today all was calm, the sea to his right gleaming like glass. A blissful silence hung over the surrounding emerald hills and seeped soothingly into his aching bones.

He'd come home.

Content at that, he gave an extravagant sigh of pleasure. This magical and beautiful county on the Atlantic coast of Ireland had stubbornly and painfully filled his dreams. Time after time he'd woken with an empty heart that hurt with the agony of longing. And now his dreams had come true.

A stupid grin softened every line of his strong-boned face. He loved this place with a passion he'd been forced to deny, ever since his unwilling and abrupt departure at the age of twenty. Wild horses wouldn't drag him away this time. This was it, for the rest of his life—and beyond.

By the post office that proudly occupied Mrs O'Grady's front room, he saw a group of people gossiping. The strange symptoms of indigestion kicked in his stomach again as he slowed, mindful of the speed limit. To his surprise, he noticed that his hands were shaking. Exhaustion, he diagnosed.

'Afternoon, Mrs O'Grady, ladies,' he called huskily as they recognised him and their mouths opened in amazement.

He smiled faintly. Of course, his sun-bleached hair had always been a give-away—and it must look more striking than usual against the Africa-derived tan.

''Tis like an angel's hair!' Mrs O'Grady had declared when he'd first appeared in the village as the FitzGeralds' charity child. Adding, more tartly, 'Pity his manners don't match! He's the divil's own and no mistake!'

Lorcan stiffened, because as he cruised by in the car he could see that Mrs O'Grady was lifting her fist to him!

'Get away with ye, Lorcan FitzGerald!' she yelled. 'Go back to the hellhole you...'

'And a pleasant day to you too!' he bit, the remainder of her words inaudible as the car window closed sharpish.

Some welcome! And he'd thought... No. Stupid to imagine that they would have forgiven or forgotten. They had long memories down here.

Breathing heavily, he took a swig from a bottle of water to quell the sensation of sickness, thinking that he ought to be thankful it wasn't a century ago. They'd have strung him up on the nearest tree for the crows to peck.

But...this long-running hostility posed problems. His questing thumb rubbed at the stubble on his chin. There might be some low-level harassment: broken windows, punctured tyres, graffiti...

He groaned. Damn it! He was too tired for all this!

Deflated, he slumped in the seat, elation giving way to utter weariness. Weeks of sensitive discussions with the Incambo government had wiped him out and he had nothing left in reserve.

Ahead, a cow ambled slowly across the unfenced road towards the strand, Ballykisteen's perfect crescent of Caribbean-white sand. He stopped the car and waited.

A chance look in the driving mirror showed first his haggard face—and then Mrs O'Grady's sturdy figure, gesticulating and yelling. His eyes flashed dangerously. She was pointing to the jagged rocks at the northern end of the bay, where his adoptive father had slipped and ended his life in the boiling sea.

'Yes—I remember! It's carved into my brain! Have you no heart, woman?' Lorcan snarled savagely under his breath and he stamped on the accelerator with a raw violence he'd never known he'd ever possessed.

It had been an accident, for Pete's sake! And yet he'd been branded as his father's killer. It wasn't true. Whatever they all believed, *it hadn't been his fault!*

The clawing nausea swirled hotly in the pit of his stomach and he frowned irritably, wondering what had caused his cast-iron digestion to go so awry. Jet lag on his jet lag, he supposed.

Saints alive, he felt terrible! Every inch of him, from muzzy brain to stiff ankles, was protesting at what he'd put his body through.

Weeks without proper sleep. A flight from Africa to the US, eighteen hours briefing colleagues on points of international law, a flight back across the Atlantic—Boston to Dublin—and then the long, slow drive across the breadth of Ireland to the coast of Connemara. No wonder he felt groggy.

But it would be worthwhile. And when his plans began to take shape he'd eradicate all the bad feeling and, he vowed grimly, he'd redeem himself in the eyes of the villagers.

Taut with anticipation, he swung the car into the entrance to Ballykisteen Manor, coasting along quietly through the landscaped gardens so that the engine could hardly be heard. It was his intention to wrap his mother in his arms and prompt an instinctive reaction from her. He didn't want to give her a chance to remember whatever poisons Harry had drip-fed into her during the intervening years.

Eagerly he leaned forward to catch his first glimpse of his beloved house. But when he did his heart stopped beating for a moment and he had to fight down the anger that rose in his chest.

Something wasn't quite right. The paintwork wasn't as pristine as it should be…and two shutters were hanging on their hinges. His keen eyes looked for betraying details and spotted a piece of guttering hanging loose—then a crumbling chimney stack.

The house still looked stunning, but it had clearly not been kept in perfect repair.

'Harry,' he muttered in annoyance. 'Letting things slide as usual!'

Grim-lipped, he cut the engine and strode to the front door, flinging it open, subconsciously remembering that no one locked anything in this part of Ireland.

'Mother!' he called into the emptiness. 'Mother!'

A pall of silence lay over the house. He went from room to room, noting with growing alarm that one or two expensive items were missing. The huge gilt mirror over the drawing-room fireplace. A Portland vase in the dining room worth conservatively thirty-five thousand pounds. One of the chandeliers in the ballroom. His heart began to thud.

How long had Harry been ill? Why were there no signs of his mother's presence? And who'd taken those valuable items?

A burglary, perhaps. Or worse…

An icy sensation ran down his spine as he realised the implications. Without checking the servants' quarters, he flew up the stairs two at a time and barged into his mother's bedroom.

There were none of her personal possessions there: no photographs, slippers, perfume or make-up. He took one look at the dust-sheeted bed and came face to face with the inevitable truth. His breath drew in sharply. His mother might not be alive.

Shocked, and near the end of his physical endurance, he staggered, crashing against one of the big internal shutters. And then he was utterly still.

Numbly he thought of the woman who'd become his mother, who'd given him a home and had loved him despite all of Harry's efforts to come between them…until her letters had stopped. It had never occurred to him that her silence could have been due to her death.

His eyes gleamed with an unfamiliar watery brilliance as he imagined her last moments. Perhaps she'd asked for him...and Harry, smug and triumphant, would have refused her request.

Lorcan's faltering hand gripped the hinged edge of the shutter in helpless frustration and grief. He should have been with his mother. Harry had banned him from setting foot in the house, but he, Lorcan, was afraid of no one and nothing, and he should have ignored that imperious edict for his mother's sake.

Waves of tiredness washed through him. He was so bushed he couldn't think straight. If he didn't lie down soon he'd fall asleep where he stood.

Then, as he lifted his heavy head, a movement in the garden outside flickered across his hazy vision.

His eyes were moist—almost as if he was crying—but he'd never cried beyond babyhood. Presumably the air-conditioning on the planes and the strain of driving had affected them.

He raised a hand that seemed reluctant to obey him and rubbed at his eyes, hoping against hope that one of the blurred figures out there was indeed his mother.

Perhaps, he thought, renewed optimism straightening his slumped and shattered body, his arrival wouldn't be steeped in sorrow after all.

CHAPTER TWO

DECLAN kissed Kathleen's cheek with brotherly concern. Anxiously she burrowed her face into the roughness of his working shirt and he hugged her. Dear Declan, who'd helped her to build up their organic business in the Manor's grounds and who'd supported her through some dire times.

'Don't be worrying now, darlin',' he said gently. 'Lorcan will be having his own life. If he did come, he'd take one look at this place and walk away, thinking it worthless.'

Somewhere a shutter banged—probably the one on its last hinges—and they both smiled ruefully at the apt timing.

'You see!' cried Declan. 'Only a complete *eejit* would want to live in a house needing an arm and a leg to keep it in working order!'

'Thanks for the compliment!' she muttered.

'Any time,' he said airily. 'Kate, this place is yours. It's gorgeous. Worth a fortune. Get that into your incredibly dim brain and stop worrying, will you?'

Affectionately she stretched up on tiptoe and kissed his massive jaw, the only bit of his face she could reach.

'You're a comfort,' she said with immense gratitude. 'God bless you, Declan O'Flaherty!'

The dogs began to bark madly with jealousy and the hens joined in with outraged clucks, making her laugh.

'Hush your noise!' scolded Declan to cover his shy pleasure. 'OK. That's enough worrying and picking for one day. I'd better collect the eggs and take these veggies to Ryan's Deli.'

She gave him a final hug, then detached herself. There were things to do. They had a business to run.

'I'm finishing that wedding cake for Nellie O'Brien but tell Bridget I'll collect Con as usual,' she said, then uttered a groan of dismay when she saw how late it was. 'Look at the time! Must dash. See you later!'

'Bye, darlin'!' he called, his deep voice ringing out across the garden.

Kathleen waved and blew extravagantly silly kisses as she raced to the back door with the yapping dogs close at her heels. To save time she hauled off Harry's old jumper and unbuttoned her shirt-cuffs as she went, knowing she'd need a quick bath before she could tackle the cake.

With muddy boots and socks left neatly by the kitchen door, she ran barefoot up the stairs, stripping off the shirt completely and unbuckling her belt. Harry's jeans fell about her ankles and for a moment she hopped awkwardly towards the luxurious bathroom in the master bedroom, one shapely leg free, the other struggling in vain to emerge as the dogs played excitedly with the flapping denim.

'What the devil are *you* doing here, running around half-naked?!' snarled an unexpected voice.

Taken unawares in the doorway, Kathleen yelped with surprise, overbalanced and thudded to the thick carpet, trapped by the overlong jeans. For a moment, as she lay there flat on her back, she saw stars.

Rubbing her head, she struggled to a sitting position and turned her horrified gaze on the man standing by the silk-draped bedroom window.

And, as she'd feared, it was Lorcan.

She sucked in a breath, stunned by the menace of his posture, her brain slowly registering the fury that burned behind his searing jade eyes.

'Are you all right?' he asked grudgingly, making no effort to help.

'No thanks to you!' she cried with spirit.

She glared, the initial dart of her glance taking in the

sublime cut of his soft linen suit—and that it was crumpled, as if he'd been sitting for some hours. Startlingly, his shirt was a banana-yellow, and open at a deeply bronzed throat, while a day's growth of beard gave him a wickedly piratical air that the sardonic curl of his mouth and flash of bared white teeth did nothing to dispel.

Her eyes widened as her survey continued more thoroughly. Over the intervening years Lorcan's body had broadened in the shoulder and narrowed at the waist and hip. His white-gold hair was now cropped close to his well-shaped head and his face was even more beautiful than ever.

But something had infuriated him and almost certainly it was her presence at Ballykisteen. She felt a stab of fear, her mouth quivering nervously at the extreme tension in his jaw. And then she became aware of a new sensation.

Perhaps it was just in her own mind and she was resurrecting memories of the few times when Lorcan had treated her like a woman and kissed her. Why she should do that at a time like this, she didn't know. But she could feel his overpowering sexuality taking hold of her and coiling like a serpent in her body, weakening her limbs alarmingly.

Hot and dizzy in an instant, she felt she'd been set on fire, as if he'd hurled a blazing torch at her and set her alight.

The dogs chose that moment to tug her jeans free, carrying them triumphantly to join the rest of her clothes at Lorcan's feet. Nervous of reclaiming them, she stood up, deciding to bluff this out with a show of confidence.

'Well?' he growled, brows hovering angrily above his glittering eyes. 'Why are you here?'

'To have a bath,' she shot back, deliberately misunderstanding him.

Her stomach did somersaults. Fear was replacing that rogue flash of desire but she wasn't sure she liked that either. Telling him why she had returned to the Manor was a petrifying prospect.

'What's wrong with your own bath?' he demanded.

'The plumbing's died a death.'

'*And* every plumber in Connemara?'

She bit her lip. He'd have to know some time. But not now. Coward! a little voice whispered.

'This is…more convenient,' she fudged.

'I'm so glad to be of service,' he drawled.

The dogs gave Lorcan the benefit of their soulful brown eyes, cocked heads and inane grins, which said, Pat me; I'm yours. He ignored them. It wasn't a good sign.

Kathleen tried to stop her teeth chattering with fear and wished she could speak, let alone come up with some clever remark to throw him off balance. Gloomily she acknowledged that she'd be rocking him on his feet soon enough.

Suddenly she realised that he was insolently inspecting the swell of her breasts—which seemed to be growing more voluptuous every second she drew breath…silly little gasping breaths, she noted to her dismay.

She groaned at her pathetic reaction to Lorcan's shockingly masculine sexuality. With infuriating stupidity, her pulse-rate hitched up a notch as, after a heart-stopping and languid tour, his gaze settled on her deep cleavage. She could hardly get her lungs to work at all.

'I believe most normal people undress in private,' he commented tautly. 'Unless they're strippers, lap dancers or total exhibitionists. Recognise yourself in any of those?'

'Certainly not! I thought the place was empty!' she snapped.

By the look on his face, he'd pigeonholed her as belonging to all three categories he'd described. Desperate to hide as much bare flesh as possible, she risked stepping forward and scooped up her clothes, hugging them tightly to her body.

'Is that so?' he drawled. 'I get the distinct impression you've made a habit of using my house.'

'I— I—'

Flustered, she pushed a shaky hand through her tumbling black hair, staring in momentary surprise at the scarlet runner bean flowers that had fluttered down as a result. She tried to appear calm, despite the booming of her heart and an extraordinary feeling that her entire body had reached melting point.

'You're trespassing,' he said coldly.

'I've done nothing wrong—!' she began.

'Do we have an hour or so for me to reel off the list?' he asked, a sarcastic twist to his hard mouth.

Kathleen fumed, her small body quivering with fury. 'You creep up here like a thief, without having the decency to warn me you were arriving—'

'Warn *you?* You're wanting my visiting card now?' he scathed. His eyes suddenly took on a steely hue. 'Listen,' he said grimly, 'I never dreamt you'd be here. Weren't you and your mother told to leave?'

'We *did*!' she yelled with heartfelt passion, grimly pleased to see the flicker of surprise in his icy eyes. '*I* came back,' she bit.

Her breathing accelerated as she wondered whether this was the moment to tell him *why* she'd returned. She swallowed, her eyes huge with apprehension. He'd go ballistic.

'We'll get to you shortly,' he promised, making it sound like a threat. 'First things first. Where is my mother? She wouldn't have let you set foot in this house, let alone use the bath to wash your grubby little body. What's happened? Is she…' His chin went up belligerently. 'Is she dead?'

'No, Lorcan!' Kathleen replied, shocked by the idea.

Although there was no change in his expression, his entire body seemed to release its tension. Kathleen realised what terrible thoughts must have been going through his mind when he'd stepped into the apparently deserted house. Sympathy touched her heart. Whatever kind of monster Lorcan might be, he'd always loved his mother dearly and treated her with kindness.

'Where is she, then?' he demanded.

'I believe she lives with her sister in Dublin,' she offered tentatively.

'Dublin? Of all the... I could have seen her!' His brows arrowed fiercely together. 'Why isn't she here?'

Kathleen winced at the barked question. 'I'm afraid that Harry and she had a falling-out some years ago.'

Lorcan muttered something under his breath. 'I thought he was behind this! Do you know what the quarrel was about?'

She nodded. 'You.'

He flinched. 'Par for the course. What particular aspect of me?'

There was a tension in his jaw, hinting that his curtness could be due to bottled-up emotions. She softened a little.

'I understand that Harry found out she'd been writing to you secretly. He burned your letters to her, then told her to get out of the house and find somewhere else to live.'

Lorcan's expletive flashed out unchecked. 'I apologise for that,' he muttered abruptly through clenched teeth. 'It's just that I can't stand the thought of that evil little swine bullying my mother...'

He clammed up, clearly too choked to go on. He had his Achilles' heel, she thought, watching him struggle with his emotions. He'd never been able to show his feelings freely—or even to admit he had a sensitive and loving side. But his adoptive mother had always been special to him.

'I'm sorry it happened too, Lorcan,' she said honestly. 'I gather your mother was very upset—'

'Upset?' he snapped. 'Of course she was! She'd lost her

home! Turned out by someone she'd adopted out of the goodness of her heart!'

'Well, yes, but that didn't bother her as much as losing your address,' she explained, remembering what Declan had told her. 'Your letters had been burnt and so she didn't know how she could ever contact you again.'

He sank wearily onto the four-poster bed as if his emotions had drained him. For a long time he just stared blindly into space. And then when he spoke it was in a low mutter that had her straining closer to hear.

'She didn't.' There was a long pause as if he was finding it difficult to speak. 'It *was* a misunderstanding, then. I thought she might have turned against me. I should have come over, but I thought…' He shook his head in self-recrimination. 'I thought she hated me. I rang people in the village and they said she despised me—but they would have heard that from Harry. If only I hadn't believed them…'

'Your mother always loved you,' Kathleen said quietly. 'She would never listen to anything bad said about you.'

And privately she mused on the blindness of a mother's love—even in the absence of a blood tie. But she understood it. You nurtured and protected your child and anyone who threatened him or her automatically became a potential enemy.

'Then she's more perceptive than most.' Lorcan scowled. 'Harry split us up, nevertheless. Evil little brute! His one aim in life was to break up loving relationships.'

Kathleen looked at him in dismay. There was a frightening venom in his tone. How was she going to get through the next hour or so of revelations without an almighty row?

Lorcan unnerved her just by sitting there. Despite the fact that he'd clearly been knocked for six, an angry tension gripped his body. His hands were actually trembling with it.

He shook his head as if it needed clearing. 'The house hasn't been properly looked after,' he said slowly.

'Harry got into debt,' she replied, dreading to be asked for details.

'Why am I not surprised?' Languidly, almost haphazardly, as if not in complete control of his movements, he rubbed the back of his neck and raised sleepy eyes to hers. 'Are you squatting, or something?' he asked heavily.

'N-no—!' she stammered, her heart in her mouth.

'Hmm. As I thought. Trespassing!'

She knew she couldn't tell him now. She wasn't prepared. 'It's a long story. It'll have to wait till I can tell you properly. Look, I'm in a rush. I must have my bath—'

'Without Declan to scrub your back?' When she blinked at his bitter remark and looked at him like an idiot, he said thickly, 'I saw you just now. You're still lovers. After all this time.'

'Lovers?' she spluttered.

'I'm not a fool, Kathleen,' he said, slurring his words badly now. 'I know love and tenderness when I see it.' As if he found it hard to focus, he frowned for a moment at the wedding ring on her finger and spoke with an effort. 'So…you two got married.'

The breath left her body. He'd jumped to the wrong conclusion! Her frightened glance flicked to the window where he'd been standing and she tried to remember what she and Dec had been doing in the garden.

Picking beans… She swallowed. Hugging. Exchanging kisses. Lorcan thought they were married, whereas… Her hands felt sticky with sweat. Oh, sweet heaven, how was she going to get out of this?

Scruff hopefully placed a soggy and chewed tennis ball between her feet and she stared at it in confusion. In the background, the tick of the grandfather clock on the landing seemed magnified. And suddenly she found a way to evade him for the time being till she found the switch that operated her brain.

'I m-must go!' she stammered in panic, shutting out the little voice that was branding her chicken-livered. 'I've got to clean up because I have a cake to decorate urgently!' she babbled in agitation, backing towards the bathroom. 'Vital I get it finished—'

'Uh. We…talk…after…'

Her eyes widened. She hadn't been imagining things. His speech had definitely thickened—and he was frowning in confusion, running a lean hand shakily through his silky hair…

She stiffened, recognising all the classic signs because she knew them so well. How could she have missed them?

'You're *drunk*!' she flung furiously.

'Uh?'

'Oh!' she cried in fury. 'You dis*gust* me!'

His body swayed and then he fell back onto the bed. 'Gorra…shleep,' he mumbled incoherently. And promptly closed his eyes, breathing in a deep and regular rhythm.

She stared in open-mouthed astonishment, unable to believe what had happened. First Harry, now him! What *was* it with the FitzGerald sons? She had to admit she was surprised he'd turned to alcohol—he'd always had nothing but contempt for people who drank too much.

But there could be no mistake. She'd been stupid not to realise earlier. In a short space of time he'd exhibited anger, lust, belligerence, bleariness, bright eyes, loss of balance and the shakes! For heaven's sake, how many clues did a girl need?

'Damn you, Lorcan FitzGerald!' she muttered furiously. 'I won't let you have this house, not in a million years! You won't run it into the ground like your lying, cheating brother!'

Seething with rage, she stormed into the bathroom and

slammed the bolt across the door, her face determined and the light of battle in her eyes. This was war.

For too long she'd experienced the effects of alcoholism at uncomfortably close quarters. Seeing Lorcan going the same way as his brother had aroused terrible memories of her life with Harry: the fear and disgust, the shame and the misery. Her hand pressed against her heaving stomach as she valiantly tried to put the past out of her mind.

And she loathed Lorcan for making her remember one of the most awful periods in her life. She let out a small groan. It could be starting all over again.

Her mouth arced in contempt. Ballykisteen didn't deserve another lurching, incompetent FitzGerald as its owner. Lorcan would find her opposing him at every step. She'd insist on her 'rights' and enlist the support of everyone in the village.

No alcoholic was going to take away her child's inheritance. Lorcan's behaviour had convinced her that she was justified in maintaining the pretence that she and Harry had been married.

But she was scared at the thought of opposing Lorcan and enduring his rages. Conor must be kept from him when he'd been drinking. She bit her lip. It would be a rocky time ahead, but she'd survive it somehow.

When she emerged a little later from the bathroom, pink and moist and swamped in Harry's towelling robe, it was to find Lorcan sleeping like a baby. The anger and contempt had been swept from his face to be replaced by a smooth serenity. The smile curving his lips looked so angelic that she felt a momentary tug on her heartstrings. But she knew better than to be fooled.

Nevertheless, she collected a couple of blankets and a downy pillow from the airing cupboard, gently slipped off his shoes and tucked him up. Out of habit she almost loosened his belt, as she'd done so many times for Harry when he'd come home drunk—the only time she'd ever touched him—but stopped herself in time, sucking in her stomach at the surge of sexual awareness which suddenly flooded through her.

This was no Harry, weak, vapid and indifferent to sex, and she'd better remember that. Lorcan could give off an aura of male sensuality even when sleeping. He was dangerous in any condition!

After gently easing the pillow beneath his head, however, she couldn't stop herself from touching him, despite knowing it was an invasion of his privacy—and even though the prospect of him waking up and discovering her absorption filled her with a nervous thrill of fear.

It was almost titillating, seeing him helpless like this. Her heart raced. Between her fingers, the strands of his Caesar-style hair felt silky and seductive. Tapering feathers of chunky white-gold tipped the edge of his smooth brow.

She stroked the warm skin of his forehead and, watching his mink-brown lashes warily, let her forefinger sweep down to admire the sculpting of his unmarked cheekbone before it wandered to the shadowed hollow beneath.

Desire brought a hard, hurting ache to her loins and she looked at his softly sculpted mouth hungrily. Too long without loving, she thought with a grimace.

And Lorcan had always held a fascination for her. He possessed an animal magnetism that had captivated all the women who came in contact with him—though his dark and dangerous reputation placed him out of bounds. And made him more fascinating than ever.

He smiled rarely—and yet he was smiling now, she noticed in pleasure, a sultry curve lifting the corners of his parted lips.

Then her eyes hardened and she stepped back, shaken by the ease with which she'd been briefly seduced. This was her enemy, not a potential lover.

'You carry on and fantasise over women and booze,' she muttered waspishly, turning away. 'I've got a campaign to plan and work to do.'

Yet the image of Lorcan, stripped of all bitterness and aggression, continued to haunt her as she quickly dressed in the housekeeper's room downstairs and then started to decorate the cake.

Was there another person beneath the prickly, defensive maverick who'd disrupted their lives so dramatically? Had she just seen the real Lorcan—someone kind and gentle, who dared not love for fear of ridicule or disappointment? Her nose wrinkled doubtfully. Perhaps even serial killers looked as sweet as candy in their sleep!

She sighed as she fixed a tiny sprig of white heather on the lower tier for luck. She'd need some herself. Lorcan would be a ruthless adversary. Unlike most people, he wasn't burdened by rules, social niceties or a conscience.

He'd want the house. And he despised her too much to even contemplate letting her continue to live in a small portion of it. The fight would be dirty. But fight she must; she had no choice. Shaking, she swallowed back the lurching fear and tried to steady her nerves.

While she worked, she forced herself to remember their last clash in detail. For eight years she'd put it from her mind, because he'd broken her heart and the memories were painful. But if she recalled his vicious behaviour, it might help her to realise what she was up against.

Her future and Conor's hung on a thread; if she lost her nerve and weakened, Lorcan would have them both for breakfast and relish every morsel.

CHAPTER THREE

SHE'D been seventeen then. Lorcan had been twenty and studying at university in Dublin. Although she was the housekeeper's daughter she'd had complete freedom of the house. Lorcan's father, Seamus FitzGerald, had been very kind to her—almost like a father.

Sometimes, when her mother had had one of her frequent migraines, Kathleen would take a sleeping bag from the servants' quarters and settle herself for the night in a spare upstairs room. This had been one of those occasions.

As she'd moved a few essentials that evening, she'd heard the sound of raised voices coming from the library and had known at once who it must be: Lorcan and Harry. Surprisingly she'd heard Seamus shouting, too.

Her heart had sunk. More rows! Lorcan had come back for the Christmas break. His parents had been justly proud of his exam success and his outstanding prowess on the sports field. They'd been so relieved that his bad reputation hadn't followed him to university that his welcome home had been like that of the prodigal son. Harry had been unbearable as a result, sulking like a child and lashing out at everyone.

And she, she'd had a blissful, precious few days with Lorcan, who'd seemed less strained than usual. He'd spent hours making secure pens for the animals she'd been nursing back to health, and had paid veterinary bills she hadn't been able to afford.

She'd felt closer to him than ever before. When his arm had gone around her companionably as they'd walked along the Famine Road, she'd been overjoyed.

It had dawned on her that he meant a great deal more to her than she'd realised. Dreamily she'd listened to his plans for the future and wondered if she could ever figure in them. She'd admired his powerfully expressed desire to specialise in law concerning children and had watched his animated, intensely passionate face with growing love.

He cared about the weak and the vulnerable. His strength would be used to help those in need. How could she not love a man like that?

The voices down in the library had reached a crescendo and Kathleen had winced on Lorcan's behalf as he and Harry tried to shout one another down.

Then suddenly Lorcan had come storming out, his face thunderous as he spun on his heel to glare at Harry and his father somewhere inside. 'You're wrong!' he roared. 'How can you listen to these lies?'

She'd never seen him so angry. White-faced and grim, he hurtled up the stairs to the landing where she stood transfixed in dismay. He didn't know she was there and for the first time she saw the world of pain behind his angry spat with Harry. And she wanted quite desperately to ease that pain.

Hampered by her sleeping bag, nightie, wash-bag and current novel, she was slow to move, and he was so preoccupied that he didn't notice she was there and cannoned into her.

'Oh!' she gasped, winded and dropping everything.

'What the—?' he said at the same time.

Instinctively he grabbed her to steady them both. For a moment she felt the full energising impact of his vigour. Then they parted, both breathing heavily.

He stood inches away, his eyes crackling with unresolved anger. 'Kathleen. I didn't see you,' he said tightly. 'Sorry. Have I hurt you?'

'No. I'm OK,' she replied. Deeply concerned, she

plucked up her courage and ventured huskily, 'You're not, though. What's the matter, Lorcan?'

'The usual,' he said bitterly. 'I caught that little rat feeding lies to Father,' he went on, his eyes bright with hurt. 'Apparently I'm the reason that two unmarried girls in the village are pregnant!'

Kathleen's eyes widened. That would be Sorcha and Ashleen. A horrible sensation of jealousy brought a sour feeling to her throat. 'But it's not true?' she probed, ashamed of her doubts.

'Of course not!' he said impatiently. 'But according to Harry I'm a walking sex machine with no control over my urges at all.'

'Why would he say that?' she asked unhappily.

'Because he hates me and wants to ruin any happiness I might find.' His voice softened as he gazed into her anxious dark eyes. 'You ought to know,' he said with quiet intimacy, 'that he's warned Father that you'll go the same way as Sorcha and Ashleen if you're not careful!'

Kathleen went scarlet with embarrassment. Harry's jealousy went too far!

'I don't want to cause trouble for you,' she said, squirming. 'Perhaps it would be better if we didn't see each other,' she added, alarmed by how miserable that made her feel.

He took a step forward and grabbed her hands. 'Haven't you enjoyed being with me?' he demanded urgently.

Her face lit up. 'Oh, yes! Very much!' She could have kicked herself. That had sounded far too eager! 'It's been OK,' she modified primly. 'But—'

'OK?' He smiled faintly. '"OK" is good enough for me, though I prefer "very much". Well, I make my own decisions now. Harry's not dictating to me who I spend my time with.' His eyes narrowed. 'Nor is Father.'

Kathleen stiffened and pulled away from him. This was

something she'd feared. 'Are you saying he disapproves of us being together?'

'Let's say he's uncomfortable with it. He's concerned as to where it'll lead.' Lorcan gave a cynical and humourless smile. 'It's not surprising under the circumstances, is it, your mother being what she is?'

Her world came crashing about her ears. She wasn't good enough for him. Her mother had been right.

For years it had been drummed into her that Lorcan and Harry were the sons—albeit adopted—of the well-connected FitzGeralds, whose pedigree went back to the twelfth century Norman invaders. FitzGerald ancestors had been virtually High Kings of Ireland. Seamus and his wife, her mother had warned, would never see her as their equal. There was no future in any relationship other than a casual one.

'Know your place,' her mother had said sternly. Kathleen was the housekeeper's daughter. And illegitimate. Not the best match for a FitzGerald.

Kathleen felt close to tears. She'd fallen in love with Lorcan only to have her dreams cruelly dashed. Of course it had been madness. He had a glittering future and would expect to marry a clever and beautiful woman who could further his career with elegant parties and sophisticated dinners.

With a heavy heart, she worked hard to hide her feelings so that he never suspected how miserable she was.

'I understand. It's not surprising,' she acknowledged neutrally.

He smiled thinly. 'You are aware of the situation, then. My father. Your mother.'

'Yes,' she said, fighting back the tears. 'Mother told me a while back.'

A quiver of pain pinched his mouth and immediately she

thought of his unhappiness instead of hers. Tentatively she touched his sleeve.

'I'm so sorry, Lorcan,' she said fervently. 'It's awful when families fall out. I wish Harry didn't resent you so much. I wish the two of you could be friends.'

'Don't waste your wishes on the impossible, Kathleen,' he said, gazing deeply into her eyes.

She smiled at him and impulsively took his hand. It felt strange, as if the sudden link had sparked off something extraordinary within her. A glow spread through her body and they both tightened their grip. Lorcan's chest rose and fell with unnatural rapidity, almost mirroring hers.

He feels it too, she thought in wonder.

'I'd do anything to bring you two together,' she said wistfully.

'That's typical of you,' he whispered, the affectionate warmth in his voice making her tremble uncontrollably. 'You're always caring for some sick animal, protecting the weak, or worrying about other people.'

His free hand smoothed back the rioting curls from her forehead and her body registered that he'd stepped closer even before that information reached her conscious mind. Every vein she possessed began to pulse with throbbing life. Briefly her head tipped back in pleasure before she forced it back again, horrified she could behave like some uninhibited hussy.

'I...'

Speech was impossible, his nearness unbearable. She moistened her dry lips with her tongue and she squirmed, blushing when his hot gaze fell to her hips, tightly sheathed in a skirt she'd outgrown.

'There's nothing special about me,' she managed eventually. 'Most people can't bear to see anyone unhappy. And they'd help animals in pain,' she said, clinging with difficulty to ordinary conversation. If only he'd stop touching her! She gave a little gasp as his fingers inquisitively toured the edge of her ear. It was getting hard to concentrate. 'Look how you defended me when I was being bullied!' she croaked.

'I couldn't resist. You were like a wounded bird,' he murmured.

The message in his eyes flustered her but she couldn't look away—nor did she want to. Now his hand had curved to the back of her neck and the pit of her loins had become as hot and molten as burning oil. Something odd had happened to her voice too, making it sound husky, as if she was deliberately trying to entice him. She made a huge effort to speak normally.

'Then you made those p-pens for…' Valiantly she battled on, desperate to hide the effect his drowsy gaze was having on her. 'For my sick animals,' she finished breathily.

There was a long and intense silence while he stared into her eyes. She felt so dizzy that her lids half-closed and she swayed towards him, her breasts brushing his chest before she realised and pulled back in shame as her nipples pinched into hard, painful buds that thrust against the thin material of her dress.

'Kathleen. I believe I could search the length and breadth of all Ireland,' he said, his voice so deep and filled with passion that it electrified her entire body, 'and I wouldn't find anyone so loving, kind or beautiful.'

Her eyes became enormous smouldering pools as the compliment sank in. 'I've never been beautiful in all my life!'

Lorcan's fingers splayed out over the back of her head. His smile devastated her with its tenderness.

'Wrong. You were beautiful when you were a shrimp of a child with your hair screwed in pigtails and glasses the size of saucepan lids,' he said, making her smile too.

'Now I know you're teasing—' she said jerkily.

'No. I'm not. You were beautiful then because you loved every living thing and had a gentle heart. But now...' Wonderingly his gaze caressed her face. 'I confess, looking at you takes my breath away,' he said softly.

Her heart lurched and prickles of heat tingled all over her skin. In his eyes was a look she hadn't seen before. With a sleepy sensuality, he studied her widened eyes, the arch of her upper lip, the full, demanding pout of its lower half.

It couldn't be true. Her head whirled with hopes. He found her attractive! Desirable, even. It was more than she could ever have imagined. At that moment she felt she'd become a woman.

'Lorcan.' Even the timbre of her voice had changed.

She wanted him to take her in his arms. Her eyes told him so.

Responding to their message, he drew their entwined hands to the small of her back and drove her against his body. Kathleen closed her eyes in bliss and lifted her face, shaken by the powerful passions that had taken hold of her.

'I want to kiss you,' he growled, adding helplessly, 'Every inch! Make love to you all night.' And he'd crushed her lips with his.

Kathleen had to stop decorating the cake for a moment. Her hands were shaking too much. For the rest of her life she'd remember the explosion of love and need within her and would regret for ever what she had done next.

Startled by the shocking urge to tear all her clothes off like a sex-mad hoyden, and invite the wicked warmth of his mouth to roam her body, she'd protected herself *from* herself in the only way she'd known how.

She'd wanted to seem sophisticated to the worldly Lorcan, not some country girl from the sticks who succumbed with a kiss, however passionate, however skilled that kiss might be. So she'd borrowed a line from a film she'd just seen.

'Hold it. I'm not going that far,' she murmured when she could draw breath, 'without a ring on my finger.'

In the film, the heroine had sashayed away, leaving the hero tearing his hair out. This, however, was reality and she was hungry for the taste of Lorcan's mouth. Her eyes flirted with his provocatively, her desire plain for him to see.

'Just kiss me, Lorcan, nothing else!' she'd pleaded huskily.

His jaw clenched hard. 'I can't. If that's all you want, I daren't continue,' he rasped, his gaze intensely hot as it toured her inviting lips. 'The way I feel, kissing wouldn't be enough for me, Kathleen. I have to be honest. My mind tells me to respect your decision. My body's driving me to seduce you. And the way I'm feeling at this moment, I know whose side I'm on.'

And as if to prove he was right to warn her, his hand was curving down the outline of her body, sweeping into her tiny waist and out again over her hips. An answering beat of need pulsed within her, shortening her breath even more.

It scared her. Before she lost her head and let him go further, she moved back.

This was pure lust and she'd been stupid to think otherwise. Her mother had warned her over and over again in bitter tones that Lorcan and Harry might try to seduce her but she'd be nothing more than a sexual convenience. Love would never enter the equation, and, even if it did, a FitzGerald would never marry a housekeeper's illegitimate daughter.

'Never, never, never!' her mother had shouted, almost hysterically.

And Kathleen simply wasn't prepared to surrender her

virginity to any man other than her husband. She took a deep breath and obeyed the cold voice of reason.

'Let's forget this happened. The truth is, Lorcan, that I want a lot more than you can give,' she grated as her dreams splintered into tiny pieces. Her head lifted proudly and she looked him straight in the eyes. 'You're not the man for me.'

He went rigid, staring at her white-lipped as if she'd slapped him on the face. Miserably she gathered the things she'd dropped and shut her door on his unnerving silence.

She flung herself on the bed and cried her heart out, sobbing hysterically into her pillow. It seemed so cruel that just when she'd realised how deeply she cared for Lorcan, she'd had to rein back her feelings.

Huddled miserably in bed in the early hours, she listened to the sounds of Harry stumbling up the stairs. With dismay, she realised he was drunk, an increasingly common occurrence. Almost certainly he'd wake Lorcan. There'd be another row. She couldn't stand that.

Quietly she crept outside. 'Shh!' she warned, pointing to Lorcan's room along the corridor.

'Kathleen! Just the person I wanted!' Harry cried in delight.

He swayed towards her, bearing her into the room till she fell back onto the bed. Covering her with his body, he began to drag up her nightie while she struggled helplessly beneath him.

When she tried to protest, his mouth clamped on hers, vile and wet. Astonishingly, he began to tickle her, and she wriggled like an eel, giggling hysterically despite her fear and anger.

Harry laughed as if he didn't care who heard him and tickled her harder. She was in the middle of a fit of breathless laughter when the light snapped on. She froze, her eyes wide with horror. Inexplicably, Harry was grinning.

Over his shoulder, her desperate eyes met those of Lorcan. She would have given anything at that moment to sink into the floor.

'*Kathleen!*'

She could hardly speak for shame. 'Don't blame Harry!' she begged. 'He—'

Harry's fingers closed on her breast in warning. She stared at his flushed and terrified face and hesitated. If she protested that he hadn't known what he was doing because he was drunk, Lorcan might tell his father.

Poor Harry already suffered because he'd disappointed his parents. He wasn't as clever or as athletic as Lorcan. High expectations had driven the miserable, awkward Harry to drink. He had an inferiority complex a mile high and she felt great pity for him.

'I'm *not* blaming him,' seethed Lorcan. 'You conniving little tramp! Did your mother put you up to this or was it your own idea?'

Harry chuckled.

'Whaaat?' she gasped.

Lorcan's mouth twisted unpleasantly. 'You made it clear that you wanted more than I could give. What was I, then? Something to practise on with your sultry looks and bed-me lips before you moved on to Harry—because he's the one who'll inherit the FitzGerald fortune?'

With an anguished cry, she pushed Harry off, pulling down her nightie under the intrusive eyes of the two brothers. She wanted to weep.

'You're talking rubbish!' she cried pitifully.

Lorcan took an angry step forward, his fists clenched. 'Am I?' he gritted. 'Your mother knows she'll never achieve her ambition to marry Father. It wouldn't surprise me if she's taught you how to twist men around your little finger instead!' he accused, his words spilling over themselves in a bitter rush. 'Adorable, vulnerable Kathleen,' he sneered, 'everybody's sweetheart. Kind to dumb animals—'

'Lorcan!' she gasped, stunned by his invective. 'How can you say such things—?'

'Because I've caught on at last!' he flung viciously. 'You deceived me. I know my father's a fool—he's even admitted as much to me—but I never thought I'd fall for the same tricks which trapped him! He advised me to tread carefully with you. I chose to ignore him and trust my instincts, more's the pity. And now *Harry's* the O'Hara victim! Harry, of all people! You make me sick!' he spat. 'You and your mother have the morals of the gutter!'

She went numb with shock, her face drawn and a sickly grey. 'My mother? What are you saying?' she cried wretchedly.

'Don't use the hurt spaniel technique on me!' he said with grim fury. 'You admitted that you understood my father's reservations about my interest in you. You know *exactly* what your mother does when she has these imaginary migraines.' His lip curled at her bewilderment. 'I *hate* it, Kathleen! I've kept quiet for my mother's sake, but it sticks in my craw to think of our housekeeper romping with my poor, besotted father and that she got her claws into him the minute she arrived eighteen years ago—'

'No!' she whispered, weak with horror.

He took a deep breath and his eyes glittered feverishly as he hurled his final arrow. '*Ask* her! I wouldn't be surprised if you're his bastard daughter!'

Now, Kathleen shakily placed the cake in a tin and went to get a glass of water. All hell had broken loose at that moment. None of them had realised that Mrs FitzGerald had been listening in the corridor, alerted by the commotion coming from the spare room. The poor woman had been unaware that her housekeeper was her husband's mistress.

It had been a well-kept secret from everyone, it seemed, other than Lorcan.

Holding the glass in two hands to stop it spilling, Kathleen drank it down, reliving the ensuing nightmare. She and her mother had been ordered to go by seven the next morning.

She'd been heartbroken. Lorcan hated and despised her. His cruel accusation had made her instantly homeless—even though she'd lived at Ballykisteen for the whole of her life. And his revelation had killed all the respect and affection she'd felt for her mother.

In addition, by a cruel trick of fate, his action had ruined the FitzGeralds' lives for ever.

With a heavy heart, she finished the rest of the cake, trying not to think of anything as she gloomily placed the model bride and groom on the top tier beneath an arch of sugar flowers. Marriage! she thought with a shudder. The heartache it brought wasn't worth it. If only she wasn't such a useless judge of men!

CHAPTER FOUR

WAKING late the next morning, Lorcan collected his suitcases from the car, bathed, changed, and headed for the
kitchen and its tempting aroma of cooking.

That would be Kathleen, he thought grimly. It was clear
she was using the Manor to squat in, the arrogant little
minx! Well, she couldn't stay in the house a moment
longer. It was out of the question.

And yet the angry words he'd prepared died before they
reached his lips. She was indeed there, tousled and rosy-
cheeked, making herself totally at home and wearing the
same enormous jumper which had made her look so vulnerable and gut-achingly sexy the day before.

And she was spoon-feeding a young child.

A shaft of emptiness opened up inside him. Answering
her muted greeting with a barely audible mutter, he sat
down suddenly at the table, grabbing a solitary slice of toast
and buttering it fiercely so that his gnawing hunger could
be satisfied. Only it wasn't. The hollow feeling remained.

'It's plain you didn't bother to eat last night,' she said
in sharp reproof when he'd demolished the toast in a few
ravenous bites. 'Black coffee's on the stove. I'll make another gallon in a moment.'

'I take tea,' he said, more grumpily than he'd intended.

'That won't help your hangover,' Kathleen said tartly.

Hastily he removed his hand from where it had been
easing the muscles at the back of his neck and embarked
on a lecture.

'You should drink water for a hangover, not coffee. It
makes too many demands on your liver,' he said.

44

'You know a lot about hangovers, then.'

'Enough to know I don't have one.'

'Could have fooled me,' she sniffed, giving him a caustic once-over. 'Still, if you want to suffer… Kettle there, teapot on the dresser, tea in the caddy.'

Without comment, he made tea and resumed his seat. He looked around, noting the signs of long-term occupation. Postcards on the fridge. Reminders on a noticeboard. A calendar filled with writing for the month—clearly a busy social life. Bully for her. In his home, too!

It would be dinner parties next, with outside caterers dishing up the latest fad and Kathleen queening it at one end of the table and Declan at the other. What a nerve!

Begrudgingly, he had to admit that the big farmhouse kitchen seemed homely and welcoming, with huge pots of foliage and luxuriant plants everywhere. It reminded him of his childhood, when he'd been treated to illicit snacks by little Kathleen and they'd nursed some animal—usually a road casualty—on the comfortable old sofa in the corner.

He allowed a half-smile to emerge for a fleeting second. A one-eared cat with straggly fur stared back at him from a box on the sofa where it nestled comfortably in the folds of a pink blanket. Not everything had changed, then.

The stainless steel sink gleamed; the antique pine furniture smelled faintly of beeswax. Photos had been propped up on the mantelpiece above the enormous turf fire. His eyes narrowed as he scanned them. There were several pictures of a dark-haired baby. Animals. Declan. Kathleen.

His heart constricted and he gulped down the tea then picked up a cereal packet with a teddy on it.

'That's Con's porridge. You won't want that. When I've finished here,' Kathleen said, sounding preoccupied, 'I'll cook something for you. You might say hello to Conor. He likes people to talk to him.'

Lorcan grunted like a bear with a sore head and did no

such thing. The child was about a year old and had Declan and Kathleen's mop of black hair, Declan's strong chin and a laughing face. Great-looking kid. The sort you'd be proud of.

He rubbed with annoyance at the pain in his chest.

Glowering, he watched the sweetness of Kathleen's expression as she transferred some orange goo into the child's eager mouth. His own mouth curled cynically. She really knew how to lay on a good softening-up scene! Any minute now there'd be a touching ballad on the radio. But if she thought he'd go weak at the knees because she was doing her Adorable Mother of the Year act, she could think again.

Sourly he wondered if she'd borrowed the baby for effect and decided even Kate wouldn't be that devious. It was hers all right. Sired by that human brickhouse Declan.

'I thought country people got up at dawn,' he said irritably, blanking out one possible reason for her late breakfast.

Kathleen raised a black eyebrow. 'Some do; we did. We've been up since six. We fed and watered the animals and did some weeding. By nine-thirty we're always back for elevenses.'

He frowned ferociously. Her gall stunned him. She didn't even sound guilty about her illicit occupation of the house! He presumed that by 'we' she was referring to Declan and herself. His hand went to the tight muscles of his neck again.

'How's your headache now?' she asked, deliberately clattering plates.

'Non-existent, fortunately,' he snapped.

'Well, isn't that lucky? I don't have to worry about noise, do I?' she murmured sweetly.

'I doubt you'd pay any attention if I said I liked quiet breakfasts,' he grunted.

'How perceptive.'

With deft efficiency she wiped Conor's face and hands, then the tray of the highchair and put plastic egg cups and spoons in front of him to play with. The child banged the spoon on the tray and laughed, its small face perfectly shaped, like Kathleen's, and with the same rosebud mouth and heart-wrenching fringe of black lashes.

'Sausages, black and white pudding, bacon, eggs, tomatoes and mushrooms do you?' she asked coolly, making him start.

'Yes...' He checked his polite thank you. He was supposed to be the resident owner, not her! 'I don't believe I'm doing this!' he muttered. But he noted with reluctant pleasure the slimness and strength of her back as she reached for a heavy frying pan on a high hook. 'You're very much at home here, aren't you?' he said tersely when she began to lay bacon on the grill.

Kathleen shot him a wary glance. 'Yes.' She resumed cooking but he noticed that her gaze was constantly returning to check on her son, who was happily smacking the egg cups with a spoon, which he then thrust out hopefully in Lorcan's direction. 'He wants you to have it,' she said flatly, slipping sausages into the pan. 'Take it, please.'

Ridiculously, Lorcan couldn't bring himself to make contact with Declan and Kate's child. He ignored the offering and shut his mind to Conor's endearing burbling. With an annoyed expression, he poured himself some tea, uncomfortably aware of the disappointment on Kathleen's hurt face.

'I'm not here to play with your kid. This is a charming scene, as I'm sure you know, but it won't wash. I want you out, Kathleen. Today.'

'I bet you do—but I'm afraid it's not that simple,' she said, looking shifty. 'There are...complications.'

'No!' he barked, making the child jump. Annoyed that

she'd made him startle the kiddie, he glared, but lowered his voice to a growl. 'It's *very* simple, Kathleen—'

'Hang on, Lorcan,' she broke in, sounding nervous—as well she might. 'Con will be having his nap soon. Wait till then and we can talk.'

'Why bother? It's crystal-clear what I'm going to say. I will tell you to get out and you'll go. Your accommodation problems are no concern of mine. Go to the Welfare Office and wave your child at them,' he said brutally, dragging his gaze away from her.

'You really are a callous brute, aren't you?' she said coldly.

Despite the frosty atmosphere, there was something disturbing about the domesticity of the scene. A kind of…heightened tension in the air. Brooding, he took a sip of tea.

'You know you have no right to be here. You and Declan and the kid will have to live somewhere else—'

'Please,' she begged, her eyes melting to a deep, liquid black. They had the same effect as a blow to his solar plexus. 'Not now. I don't want Conor upset. Be patient and we'll talk. For me.' She did the eyelash thing, fluttering them prettily. And he could have sworn she'd found some tears from somewhere because her eyes were glistening. 'For old times' sake,' she pleaded.

Furious at her manipulation, he put down his cup sharply. 'Would that be the old times when you were kissing me outside your bedroom and sighing with pleasure? Or rolling in bed with my brother a few hours later? Or perhaps when you flung yourself into Declan's arms the very next morning?'

She stiffened with shock at his last accusation, clearly dismayed that he'd seen that private moment so long ago. Red-faced, she said jerkily, 'I—I was saying goodbye to Dec!'

'Yeah. As in "Goodbye lover-boy, see you later".' He fixed her with his angry glare. 'He was your lover then and—'

'That's not true!' she cried spiritedly.

'I'm a lawyer. I go by evidence. And that points to a woman with a high sex drive but an even greater ambition to better herself.'

'You're wrong!' she said, with a convincing stab at outraged innocence.

'Am I? See it from where I'm standing,' he said, having had years to work out the most likely explanation. Years of nights awake and thinking in the dark, wondering, hating. He fixed her with a look of contempt as he outlined his theory. 'Your sexual needs got the better of you and you ended up in a clinch with me. Then you remembered in time that I couldn't give you what you wanted—but Harry could. However, you knew that your chances to land Harry would be nil if he'd ever discovered that you'd played around with me. So you quickly lured Harry into your bed—'

'He was *tickling* me!' she interrupted indignantly.

Lorcan shrugged. 'That's hardly an excuse. You two were certainly having a great time. The last time I saw Harry so animated, he'd just smashed me with a spade.'

'Lorcan!' she cried, shocked.

'Later,' he went on relentlessly, 'when I'd scuttled your attempt to secure Ballykisteen, you flung yourself into lover-boy Declan's arms—probably asking for bed and board, since you had nowhere to live.' He grunted. 'You're quite something,' he said scathingly. 'Three men knocked sideways in the space of twelve hours!'

'Talk about circumstantial evidence!' she flared.

'Fact,' he countered, hard-eyed.

'Distortion,' she corrected. 'You've clearly fabricated a

case against me with the slimmest of evidence and I know it looks bad—'

'*Looks* bad?' He snorted. 'It is bad.'

'I don't want to discuss it now. Let me explain later!' she pleaded.

'It's no use looking tragic. You won't wriggle out of this, whatever wiles you use on me,' he said coldly.

Lorcan saw her small white teeth dig into her lip. She continued cooking in silence, breaking off now and then to return the things that Conor flung cheerfully to the floor.

Sometimes she'd absently kiss her son's pink cheek and would be rewarded by an answering kiss and two chubby arms around her neck.

He felt unaccountably sad. When she talked to her child she looked like the gentle and loving Kathleen he'd once known before her enterprising mother had corrupted her.

As soon as her back was turned again, he found himself studying her carefully. She'd twisted her hair into a scrunched pink band thing, which presumably had elastic in it because it managed somehow to hold her vigorous waves in check. Glossy black tendrils dangled and danced appealingly as she moved, and here and there her hair and neck were adorned with two dots of something white and sticky, perhaps the teddy bear porridge.

A lurch of affection hit him hard in the depths of his chest and he scowled. She wasn't the sweet little thing he'd imagined. Never had been. He was getting disgustingly sentimental. It was a luxury he couldn't afford.

'Full Irish breakfast.' Deadpan, her mouth downturned but still lush, she slid the plate in front of him.

'Thanks. Looks good,' he admitted.

Her fingers hooked a curl behind an impossibly cute ear. 'It's a work of art,' she said grumpily.

Starving, he tried one of the sausages. In astonishment, he attacked the succulent white pudding with equal enthusiasm. Fabulous. Fat orange yolks to the eggs, tomatoes with that old-fashioned thing called *taste*...

'It's fantastic!' he declared grudgingly.

'Of course it is!' she said, with an unconsciously haughty sway of her hips.

Lorcan sucked in his breath sharply as a shocking chauvinist thought flashed across his mind. Kathleen, barefoot and eager, serving his needs in the kitchen and bedroom. Well, judging by its instant reaction, his body approved of that idea. If it could speak, it would be offering her the post of housekeeper and mistress right now.

Ruefully he reflected that perhaps he understood his father's behaviour for the first time. The idea had a certain base appeal! And yet...he wanted more. He'd always wanted more than any woman could give.

Some of the women who'd passed through his life had been stunningly beautiful. Some clever. One or two had had ideals like his. A few had had warmth. He'd made a relationship with two but none had touched his heart, only Kathleen—but he'd been twenty then and easily deceived into thinking she was special.

'Something wrong?' she asked.

His mind took control of his useless dreams and invented a reason for staring hypnotically at his plate.

'Why don't I taste food like this in Boston?'

'*Boston?* Is that where you live?' Kathleen flipped a slender finger up and down over her lips to amuse Conor, who enchanted Lorcan by trying to mimic her. 'Perhaps you've never tasted organic meat,' she suggested uninterestedly.

He had to concede that it was the best breakfast he'd ever eaten. She watched without speaking while he demolished everything on his plate, supplying him with toast and tea till he leaned back with a sigh. That ought to sort his wayward digestion, he thought.

Avidly his eyes followed her supple movements as she

bent to throw a couple of slabs of peat on the fire. He had other needs, too. They'd not been so insistent before. But he wasn't going to make the same mistake as his father by inviting a scarlet O'Hara into his life!

'I'm going to get Conor to sleep now,' she said edgily, busying herself with the restraining harness on the highchair. 'Stay quiet till I do—once he's off, we could drop bombs around him and he'd never hear.'

When she turned to the child, the tension eased from her face. Adoration glistened in her eyes when she held the child to her breast and rocked him gently, the lush dark sweep of her lashes and sweetly tender curve of her mouth making his pulses beat heavily.

She could still turn a man's head, he thought grimly, crushing the unbearably fierce leap of desire in his loins. And she'd be willing. She was that sort. But she was married, and before he knew it she'd turn him into an adulterer. The sooner he evicted her the better.

'The child's asleep. Let's get on with it,' he said shortly, needing to rid himself of the painful sight of mother and baby together.

Her eyes met his. She seemed scared. 'All right,' she said in a choked voice.

With great reluctance, she put her son in a baby buggy, deftly manipulating catches on the back with one hand so that the seat lowered to a reclining position. He realised with surprise that motherhood in the western world brought with it a huge range of skills of which he was entirely ignorant.

When she went into what had used to be the housekeeper's quarters next door he rose curiously and looked over her shoulder while she folded and stored some baby clothes.

He stiffened. Inside was a double bed—the same one his father and Mrs O'Hara had used. There was a man's jumper on a chair and some feminine underwear. Soft toys cuddled together in some kind of small hammock affair on the wall.

Kathleen's love-nest.

How dared she? he thought, turning away in a blind rage. She and Declan had no right to be here at all! Presumably they'd been living in the gardener's cottage till Harry died, then they'd moved into the house like descending locusts! It was outrageous. The woman was amoral.

He spun round on his heel when she came back into the kitchen with a net, which she attached to the front of the buggy.

'Ready?' he barked, when she'd returned from parking Conor outside, safely within view of the full-length French doors.

She flinched, as well she might, but he was seething with an almost uncontrollable anger and had no intention of making this easy for her.

'I am, but are you fully kitted up? I see no interrogation lamp, thumbscrews and rack,' she said in tart defiance.

But when she sat down at the table and looked at him expectantly, her eyes were as black as night and she was clearly nervous.

'I can get the result I want without force,' he retorted coldly, ignoring a marmalade cat, who was purring like a steam engine by his legs and trying to attract his attention. 'I have the law on my side.'

She gave a little shudder which trembled through the length of her curvaceous body, attracting his eyes to every inch, every dip and swell. It seemed close in the kitchen, perhaps from the heat of the fire and the stove. Lorcan hauled off his scarlet sweater and moved around restlessly, trying to keep the lid on his temper.

But he kept seeing images of Kathleen and Declan in that bed together and his chest had constricted so much he could hardly breathe.

Kathleen watched him nervously, trying to gauge his mood. His face was clean-shaven now and emphasised his striking bone structure and the slash of his scar. There was a hardness about his expression. Clearly he was on the edge of an explosion and she dreaded being the object of his contempt again.

She swallowed. Sooner said, sooner over with.

'You know about Harry's death, obviously—' she began coolly.

'I wouldn't be here otherwise.'

His profile was, to her, sharp, clear and ruthless. She watched him inspecting a photo of Kieran and comparing it with one of Conor. Her heart pounded when he frowned, perplexed by the difference. She wouldn't tell him. It was too painful. Only Harry had known about Kieran.

'Presumably,' she said, leaping up and diverting his attention with an enquiring smile, 'you saw the announcement—and my advert?'

He put down the photo and turned to face her, his lean thumbs curled around his belt hooks.

'No. I've been in Africa for the past six months.'

'I thought you said Boston?' Her forehead wrinkled in confusion.

'That's my—*was* my—home base. I'm an international lawyer. I have to go abroad frequently.'

She didn't like the 'was'. But she made no comment. And she felt disappointed that he had scorned his plan to work for children in favour of a glittering career.

It wasn't surprising. He didn't like children. He'd made no effort for Con. How awful! She felt worried. When Lorcan found out who Conor's father was, he'd like him even less.

'I don't understand,' she said, spinning out the awful moment to come, 'how you heard about Harry.'

He was wandering the room again. 'One of my colleagues was flicking through the back numbers of the *Irish Times* that are sent to my Boston office and found the announcement. She rang me in Africa and I came at once. How did Harry die?'

She blinked at his quick-fire delivery. It was to confuse her, of course, a technique he'd learned in court. Well she wouldn't be thrown off balance by it.

'Harry was an alcoholic—'

'I know.'

Kathleen's mouth opened in astonishment. 'But…no one knew except the doctor and me!'

'I watch people. I notice things,' he said grimly, pausing by the wide windowsill.

Marmalade jumped up to the sill and rubbed against Lorcan's waist but he wasn't to be diverted. He assessed Kathleen speculatively.

Afraid he was systematically reading her mind with those sharp, critical eyes of his, she looked hastily away, her fingers twisting anxiously in front of her.

'His drinking got worse. He developed circulation problems,' she said flatly, keeping the information to the bare facts so she didn't disgrace herself by bursting into tears at the sheer awfulness of remembering. 'The side effects from the drugs he was taking for that, gave him kidney problems. Drugs for his kidneys affected his liver. He died of kidney failure—but the real cause was drink.' And low self-esteem before that, she thought sadly.

To her surprise, Lorcan seemed moved. 'What a foul way to go,' he said quietly. He scanned the room, focusing with hawk eyes on the small telltale signs that betrayed the years of neglected maintenance. Frowning at the mould stain over the chimney-breast, he said, 'I assume he was ill for some time.'

'To be honest, things were bad from the start. Harry couldn't cope with managing the house and land at all,' she told him, her pained eyes betraying some hint of the horror she'd gone through. Carefully skipping the treatment which had bankrupted Harry, she said, 'He built up debts and he drank even more to escape reality.'

On an impulse, she went to the dresser and pulled out a drawer, searching through it till she found a picture of Harry. Lorcan might as well see what drink could do to a man.

'Here.'

'Harry?' he rasped in disbelief.

When she nodded, he studied the photograph again, his face plainly showing what he thought of the transformation. Harry had always been on the plump side, but never as bloated as in the year before his death. He'd been snapped with newborn Con in his arms and the contrast between the perfect little face and Harry's coarsened red features would have shocked anyone. His hair was lank, his clothes unkempt. And Kathleen vividly remembered being loath to hand her beautiful Con over to him.

'What was he, godfather?' Lorcan asked.

'No.' She changed the subject, still too chicken to tell him. 'He got worse than that as his drinking progressed,' she said, determined to make Lorcan face up to his own failing.

Lorcan irritably brushed cat hairs off his pink shirt, moved away from her to lean against the dresser, and folded his arms. Remorselessly his eyes bored into hers.

'I suppose that's why you were horrified when you thought I was drunk last night,' he commented with typically shrewd perception.

Her mouth tightened. If he was going to pretend he'd been stone-cold sober, she wasn't!

'I didn't *think*. You *were*. I'm an expert in reading the signs. And Ballykisteen needs a drunken owner like it needs a hole in the roof!' she cried passionately. 'It needs love and care and money—'

'Exactly. And I'm here to provide that. I know how much it costs to keep up a house like this. Even you, with all your talents, couldn't earn enough for routine maintenance,' he said sarcastically. 'We're talking big money here. My sort of money.'

'Huh! You'll destroy it like Harry!' she blurted out.

'What I do is none of your business!' he retorted, his eyes blazing angrily. 'Besides, you don't seem to be doing much—'

'I'm giving it everything I've got!' she cried heatedly, her fists tightly clenched. 'I pour every penny I can into it! I love Ballykisteen—*and* I'm sober in my spare time and—'

'I'm not an alcoholic, Kathleen,' he said quietly. 'I was tired, not drunk. I've flown halfway across the world and slept very little in the past three days.'

She let her doubts show. Harry had deluded himself that he'd 'never been drunk' too. Surely a flight from Boston didn't turn a fit young male into a slurred, staggering zombie?

'I hope you've recovered from your exhausting journey,' she clipped.

Lorcan ignored her sarcasm, his eyes sharp and cynical. 'Perfectly. So let's get down to business. What exactly are you doing here? Pretending you're lady of the manor? Living out the fantasy you always wanted to achieve but couldn't?'

Kathleen sat down in defeat, her knees suddenly useless. If he was annoyed that she might be *playing* lady of the manor, how would he react when she told him she *was*?

'Ladies don't dress like this and spend their days in the garden stuffing soil up their fingernails,' she muttered sulkily.

'Then explain.'

'Dec and I run an organic fruit and vegetable business.'

'From *here*? You're using *this* land for *your* business?' He flashed a look out of the window at the regimentally neat rows of vegetables and fruit bushes. 'Well, thank you,' he said sardonically. 'It's just what I've always wanted. You've saved me from creating my own kitchen garden.'

She bridled. If he thought he was taking over her pride and joy, he was mistaken! 'It is looking good,' she agreed, trying to keep her tone even. 'We use the west meadow, too. We've begun to build up profits. It's a premium price business—'

'Who are your customers?'

'Local cafés and restaurants. We're in great demand. And we make up boxes for retail sale—'

'How long's it been operating?'

'Four years…'

She faltered. Lorcan had gone white around the lips.

'I don't believe this!' he seethed. 'You must have been operating under Harry's nose?!'

'Ye-es, but—'

'Dammit, woman, you took advantage of a drunk to hijack his land and carve out a living for you and your lover!'

'He's not my lover!' she snapped.

'Oh, my apologies. *Husband*. You two have certainly grasped your opportunity, haven't you?' he finished with blistering contempt.

Her hands clenched. Here goes, she thought, a terrible sinking sensation burning into the pit of her stomach.

'Declan…isn't my husband,' she said in a barely audible whisper.

CHAPTER FIVE

LORCAN straightened as if she'd shot a bolt of lightning through his spine. 'Say that again!' he grated menacingly.

She was hypnotised by the extraordinary stormy colour of his eyes. Her knees began to knock.

'Declan's married to Bridget Mulligan, the baker's daughter,' she said faintly.

'Bridget!'

'They—they were wed about seven years ago,' she stumbled on.

'Children?'

'Yes,' she mumbled. 'Two—'

'You poisonous little trollop!' he hissed. 'He's a married man with children and *still* you fling yourself at him!' She flinched from his anger, cringing away, and his eyes narrowed shrewdly. 'What is it?' he demanded. 'You thought I was going to hit you, didn't you? How dare you? I've only ever hit Harry, and that was in self-defence,' he said tightly.

She snorted. 'He said you'd gone for him with a spade and swung it so wildly that you hit yourself. And then you punched him in temper.'

'I know what he said. That doesn't mean his version is true.' Lorcan's eyes gleamed. 'People always believed his lies. Which one of us pulled the legs off spiders, Kathleen? Who maltreated any animal and person smaller than him?'

She bit her lip. 'Harry.'

'And who protected cats and dogs and the underdog from his twisted sadism?'

'You,' she whispered, ashamed.

59

'At last!' he scorned. 'Someone other than my mother believes me. And it has to be you, a cheating little tramp. What do you want from life, Kathleen? What will satisfy that ego, that huge sexual appetite of yours?' he goaded. 'Every man on this earth panting for you? You're not fit to be a mother. I can't believe I ever—'

His mouth clamped shut suddenly and with an exclamation of disgust he turned his back on her as if he couldn't bear the sight of her.

Close to tears, Kathleen stared at the tense musculature of his furious back. She didn't want him to think badly of her. It hurt. There was a terrible pain in her heart as if his opinion mattered…as if she cared about him. Perhaps he was half right. She wanted to be liked by people. But was that so dreadful?

'Lorcan,' she mumbled miserably, her fingers reaching out to alight uncertainly on the soft fabric of his shirt.

He recoiled violently as if she'd stabbed him. 'Don't *touch* me!'

'I—I wanted to apologise for thinking that you might hit me,' she said jerkily, trying to forget the gut-wrenching fear which had hammered in her brain.

Slowly he turned, his mouth grim. 'It was instinctive, wasn't it? Someone's been violent with you, to elicit that knee-jerk response. Who was it? Declan?' he rapped.

'Absolutely not!' she cried, scandalised. 'Dec's a sweetie—'

'Tell his wife, not me,' he snarled. His glittering green eyes narrowed shrewdly. 'Who was it, then?'

She knew it would be a mistake to answer. 'Just a minute. First you must let me defend myself about my relationship with Dec,' she pleaded. 'A court of law would give me that right.'

'You forget. I saw what you were doing with him yesterday, Kathleen!' he bit out. 'Hugs and kisses and "darlin's" were being flung about to the four winds.'

She tried to keep calm, despite the panic that made her voice sound horribly breathy. 'There's nothing in it. We're like that together. Jokey. Friends,' she protested, her eyes huge as she looked at him.

'Yeah. Bosom pals. Always have been, haven't you? Making fools of the FitzGeralds like your damn mother.'

She felt the pricking of tears and brushed them away with her knuckles. When she focused again from beneath spiky dark lashes, Lorcan looked even angrier.

'You must believe me!' she insisted brokenly. 'When you saw us yesterday, I was upset. He cares about me. We do love each other,' she conceded, deciding to tell him their true relationship. 'But it's not what—'

'Spare me! I've seen you in too many men's arms to be convinced by your innocent indignation.' His mouth firmed into an uncompromising line and in her anger she decided to let him think what the devil he liked. 'Just who *is* your poor, deluded husband?' he asked coolly. 'Perhaps I should buy him a consoling drink.'

This was it. She took a deep breath to steady her nerves.

'Not who is. Who…who *was*,' she corrected huskily, stopping short of adding the lying words 'my husband'.

And he was quick. His mind had always been sharp. Realisation was dawning; she could see that from his horrified expression. With a shaking hand he dragged out a chair and virtually sank onto it, staring at her in numb disbelief.

'*Harry?*' he asked in a hoarse croak.

Kathleen lowered her guilty eyes and kept them fixed on her fingers, which were twisting and turning her wedding ring. 'Harry.'

'And he was the one who slapped you around.' When she didn't answer, her face so miserable that the truth was obvious, he drew in a harsh breath and muttered a profanity. '*Did* he hit you?' he enquired tightly.

'Not exactly. He usually missed,' she said in a pathetic little voice.

His teeth ground together. 'Little rat! He never tackled anyone his own size! How he could…' He bit back whatever he was going to say and stared at her. 'I can't believe it. You…Harry's wife!' He looked shattered by the news, his eyes icy green as he ground out, 'So you succeeded in landing him, then, as you'd always intended.'

The depths of his loathing and contempt shook her to the core. She could feel the pain of his disgust sucking the life from her body. The tension strung out her nerves till she thought she might scream for release.

'It wasn't like that, Lorcan,' she whispered, sick at heart.

'No. Of course not. You two fell in love, got married, the earth moved… Do you think I'm stupid, Kathleen? You're no grieving widow. You never cared for him. How could you?' He picked up Harry's photo and held it so she was forced to look at it. 'You loved this? You: soft as putty, so soft that you need a lorry-load of tissues even to watch the opening titles of *Bambi*, and Harry: an evil-minded, twisted, bitter drunk who got his kicks out of torturing animals and people alike? I don't think so!'

She turned her head away, aghast at his analysis, her hand over her mouth to hold back the nausea. How had it all happened? How had Harry stopped drinking long enough to persuade her with his undoubted charm that their secret and mutually convenient arrangement could ever work?

'What was the attraction? Tell me,' he said mockingly.

Trying to sort things out in her own mind, she began to speak in a low, mechanical tone, her body limp and lifeless.

'After he turned your mother out of Ballykisteen,' she

explained, 'Harry came to London to find me. Declan knew where I was staying—'

'I bet!' Lorcan growled sarcastically.

Somehow she continued. 'Harry...made a proposal.'

'And you accepted like a shot!' he rapped in scalding contempt.

She flinched, wishing she could tell him the truth and earn his understanding instead of his hatred.

It hadn't been a marriage proposal. Her acceptance had, in fact, been the result of hours of agonising and she had no intention of explaining why. Nor would she tell him of the strict conditions she'd imposed. It was better he didn't know.

Kathleen worked at the hard lump in her throat. Silence built up again, heavy and pressing. Her hands clutched tightly together against her chest while he just sat there like a stone without even blinking, as if her revelation had robbed him of energy too.

His stillness was unnerving her. She felt a powerful urge to blurt out the facts. That she'd been married at eighteen, an innocent abroad in London. That her child had been taken from her to a foreign country where he'd died. She'd been emotionally vulnerable, mourning her baby and desperately homesick. Harry had offered her a lifeline.

Wouldn't Lorcan understand then? It was terrible to live the lie. It was burning her tongue.

And yet somehow she managed to stop herself. She had to keep up the pretence that she'd been married. Lorcan hated her so much that he wouldn't hesitate to bring all his legal expertise to bear on the matter and evict her on the flimsiest pretext.

She raised brimming eyes to Lorcan. 'Don't condemn me,' she begged brokenly. 'You don't know the circumstances—'

'You married Harry,' Lorcan muttered, his face suddenly

haggard. 'And now he's dead. Ballykisteen is yours when I'd thought it was mine. Astonishing luck on your part—or was it judgement? My congratulations. I admire your cunning, even if I can't bring myself to applaud your morals.' He rubbed his temple as if it ached. 'The Manor is yours,' he said dully. 'Yours!'

She ignored his sneer. He looked devastated—and amazingly her one thought was to reassure him. 'It isn't. Not entirely. That's the problem I was telling you about, Lorcan,' she said quietly, her conscience hurting her unbearably because he looked shattered, as if she'd just trampled on his most cherished dreams.

He sat up, instantly alert and hopeful. 'He's mortgaged it? The mortgage company owns it?'

'No. Harry left the estate to me and you, to be shared equally.'

'Like hell he did!' he scoffed.

'Do you think I'd make up something like that?' she asked bitterly. 'Read the will if you like. It's in the desk. Do you imagine for one second that I would ever *want* to share it with you?'

He stared at her resentful face for several seconds, the truth quickly dawning on him. Plainly stunned, he sat back tensely in the chair and she watched in grudging awe while he adjusted with unnerving speed to the new situation.

When he met her eyes again it was with a new confidence, as if he'd analysed all the angles and had decided which solution suited him best.

He was yet to learn she wasn't a push-over! she thought, preparing herself for his next move.

'This changes the situation completely.'

His voice had been velvety and soft, slipping under her defences seductively. Before she knew it, he had drawn his chair around the table so that they were almost knee to knee.

His powerful presence swamped her in an instant and all she could think of was the appealing breadth of his chest, the narrowness of his waist, and the mist descending on her brain.

It was unbelievable. In the midst of all this, her body chose to think of its own selfish needs! Angrily she forced her fluttering hands to be still and took several oxygenating breaths.

'It means we're equal,' she said in a shaming croak.

He smiled, startling her. 'That's right. We share this house, you and me.'

It seemed almost carnal, the way he said it. She felt her pulses beating rapidly at the implied intimacy.

'In theory but never in practice, I presume,' she said as casually as she could when her heart seemed determined to lurch up to her throat.

Her eyes dropped from his faintly smiling mouth to his hands, which rested on his knees. Mesmerised, she watched as one of those hands lifted and came to land on her thigh.

'The situation is straightforward. You've got something I want.' The warmth of his fingers seeped into her flesh and it took all her will-power to push his hand away. 'I mean to have it.'

Kathleen swallowed, astonished by the rivers of heat running through her. Sucking in a deep breath, she pressed her knees tightly together and focused blankly on his stomach.

'You can't want the hassle of this place—'

'Surely that must go for you too?' he asked mildly. 'I have the solution. I'll buy you out.'

The soft approach, she thought. He was going to play the Mr Nice game in an attempt to charm her. 'No. This is my home and Conor's. We're not budging!' she declared firmly.

He leaned forward and she was trapped by the intense look in his eyes. 'I'm sure you'd like to sell for a good price,' he purred, persuasion itself. 'It would be such a good opportunity, wouldn't it? To have enough money to go abroad, to start a new life—'

'I'd never leave Connemara!' she replied, her brain oddly turgid.

Lorcan's eyes flickered with irritation. 'You intend to stay, whatever happens?'

'Whatever happens!' she replied with heartfelt passion.

Between them hung a languid and sultry pause during which he seemed to be raking every inch of her face with interest. Sexual interest.

She quivered and tensed. His eyes had become hooded and drowsy and were fixed on her pouting mouth. Instantly she felt a spasm which contracted the peaks of her breasts, then drew in her stomach and scythed into her womb.

To her horror, she saw that he had noticed her involuntary flinch, and the slow, knowing smile that curved his lips made her colour up in shame.

'Then we have a problem. It must be clear to you that we can't live in the same house, Kathleen,' he commented, his eyes lazily seductive. 'We'd either end up trying to murder one another...or in bed making love.'

His outrageous claim had startled her so much that she couldn't speak for a moment. It was true, she thought in dismay. There was something electric happening between them. She could feel the drift of his breath over her mouth and smell the maleness of him and knew that her whole body was screaming out for his touch even though he was her worst enemy.

'Murder, possibly. Bed, never!' she said coldly, but the effect was spoiled by the wobble in her voice.

His eyes glittered. 'Perhaps you're right.' He drawled the words languorously, as if he knew otherwise.

Annoyed to be linking Lorcan and bed together—and finding her heart-rate had shot into the stratosphere as a result—she gritted her teeth and ignored the deliciously illicit sensation that had attacked her limbs.

She had to concentrate on the problem and put all unnecessary thoughts of Lorcan out of her mind. Her future depended on this.

After a moment of desperate thought a solution proposed itself. 'Lorcan,' she announced in relief, 'you must be the one to go.'

'Why?'

'Because,' she said smugly, 'it would take a sadistic monster to turn out a defenceless widow and her child.'

She'd done it! Presented him with a situation he couldn't handle! Fizzing with delight and a sudden burst of energy, she stood up, intending to clear the plates.

He looked annoyed at her tactics but his eyes were sharp and his mouth determined as he said smoothly, 'You're right—though I have to tell you that it wouldn't bother me at all to *be* that sadistic monster—'

'And suffer the hatred of the whole village?' she asked with great satisfaction. Get out of that one! she thought.

He gave a faint smile. 'I agree, that's the only thing that would give me pause for thought,' he admitted. And as she looked at him, unable to keep the pleasure of victory from her face, he murmured, 'However, I could save that poor, defenceless widow and her starving child from a life of constant struggle. I'd offer her a vulgar amount of money to buy her out. That would go down well at the post office. I'd be a hero in Mrs O'Grady's eyes,' he added, his intense gaze taunting her.

'But I've told you, I'm refusing your offer—' she began uncertainly.

'Yes. And how will that look, when it's known that you turned down such a chance? What would people think of you for letting your stubborn pride keep you and your son in a state of poverty, when you could both be living very comfortably in a smart new bungalow in the village?'

'I hate bungalows!' she muttered.

'That's not the point, is it, Kathleen?' he said silkily.

She glared, but inside she was quaking. He was clever, turning her own gibe against her. Serve her right for using Conor to blackmail him.

Breathing heavily, she doggedly began to clear the breakfast table.

Her tongue slicked over her dry lips. He'd out-manoeuvred her. She racked her brains to come up with a new attack, formulated it, and shot him a quick glance. He looked amused and smug—but she'd wipe that smile off his face!

'I assume you wouldn't let Declan and me work the veg garden?' she asked casually, running water into the sink.

'You're damn right I wouldn't!' Lorcan growled with unusual vehemence.

'Oh, dear,' she sighed extravagantly. 'So he will be out of work—and what would happen to his family? Bridget, with a daughter aged four *and* a year-old baby?' she cooed. She turned to face him, soapy hands on her hips. 'What *will* the village think of you? Supposing the local papers got wind of this! There could even be a campaign. Placards. Graffiti. That kind of thing.'

'What a devious and clever woman you are,' he said icily.

'I'm only stating the truth. We must stick to facts, mustn't we? We're back to sadistic monsters, I think.' She heaped troubles on his head with a grim glee. 'And there's Kevin, of course.'

Lorcan sardonically lifted his eyes to heaven and sighed. 'Another of your lovers with a wife and young family?'

'No wife, no family. He works for us, making cakes and pastries in the bakery, which we sell on at our outlets,' she said jauntily, sure now that Lorcan would run a mile rather than cause trouble for Kevin. She gave a disarming smile and cocked her head on one side. 'You remember?' she purred, almost enjoying herself now. 'Kevin O'Grady?'

Apparently he did. Lorcan was looking daggers at her because he knew that big Kevin was thirty-four with a mental age of eight and a wonderful way with ponies and pastry alike.

Her eyes sparkled as her heart-rate increased with excitement. Perhaps she'd got the better of Lorcan!

'I'll employ him. And...Declan,' he said grudgingly, his eyes lingering on her curving mouth. 'But not you. Not ever.'

Her hopes collapsed. She banged the frying pan noisily on the draining board. Now what? Licking his boots?

'I imagine you're wealthy enough to be comfortably settled in Boston,' she said crossly. 'What would *you* want with a house with bad memories?'

'Because I *love* it!' he said quietly. 'Every stick and stone. It was my first real home after being pushed from one children's home to another, then from foster parent to foster parent. Life wasn't terrific here but it was stable. And—' His voice lowered to a whisper. 'I did find love— for a brief time.'

Her heart lurched at the intensity of his feelings. For the first time she understood why his adoptive mother had been so important to him. No one else had shown Lorcan so much love.

She looked at him in dismay, reluctant to pursue her course in the face of such a reason. But she must. For Conor.

'Now come on, Lorcan,' she coaxed. 'It would be impossible for you to settle here. The villagers would make your life very difficult. Go back to Boston. Forget Ballykisteen—'

'I wish I could!' he said fervently. 'But ever since I left I've been determined to return. I will not give up my decision to live here, Kathleen, and I'm confident the villagers will change their minds about me. I have important plans for the house.'

'Plans!' she cried, pouncing on the word in alarm. 'What plans? You can't alter it—'

'I will do what I want! For heaven's sake, see sense. It's a tremendous responsibility. You can't possibly afford its upkeep and it'll gradually deteriorate. Here—' He dragged a chequebook from the back pocket of his black jeans and opened it.

'You're not listening to me!' she cried desperately. 'I won't go!'

'Oh, I think you will,' he said through his teeth.

'Wait and see!' she muttered, visions of chaining herself to the bedpost going through her mind. And then something sexier came into her head. Related to bed again. And Lorcan.

Simmering with unusable carnal energies, she gave the frying pan a good seeing to with the scouring pad.

There came a soft thud as he flicked the chequebook across the table. 'This is what I'm offering you. The amount will go down by a thousand pounds a day as an inducement not to delay. Accept now and you and your illegitimate child—'

'How *dare* you?' she flared, whirling around in shock. Did he know? Her son. Illegitimate. She'd never thought of it like that before. It sounded vile. She stared at him white-faced. 'Why…why do you use that word about Conor?'

'He sure as hell doesn't look like Harry!' he snapped back. 'Odd that he's the spitting image of Declan!'

She gasped. 'That's outrageous!' she cried. Hadn't she

gone through a nightmare to produce an heir for Harry? 'He's Harry's, I swear!'

'You may have fooled him,' Lorcan said scornfully, 'but not me.' He stood up abruptly. 'I want to see the will. After that, you can tell me what you've done with several valuable objects that are missing. I want them back.'

'I don't know where they are. Harry sold them. His papers are in that desk over there. I haven't had time to sort it out; it's in such a mess.' Mutinously she glared at him. 'Don't get too excited about any legacy you're expecting. You've inherited nothing but debts.'

'Then so have you,' he said tightly. 'All the more reason to take the money and go. Leave me to worry about the debts.'

Her small, hot face tipped up proudly. 'I can't be bought!'

In two strides he'd crossed to the sink where she stood and had trapped her there, leaning menacingly over her as his hands slammed down on the draining board either side of her trembling body.

'*Harry* bought you!' he hurled hotly, his face close enough for her to feel the branding flame of breath across her mouth. 'He paid for your body and you sold yourself to him!'

'Please, Lorcan! Don't say such things!' she begged, miserable because it was true in a terrible way.

'You wanted the Manor and to be a FitzGerald. Marrying Harry was the price you had to pay! My God! Your mother must be proud of you! She only achieved mistress status!' he scathed. He seared her with a killing glance. 'But then she'd been training you up for years, hadn't she?'

'That's ridiculous! I didn't even *know* she was your father's mistress till you yelled it to all and sundry!' she defied, pressing back from his intimidating body into the hard edge of the draining board. 'I was shocked *rigid*. And yet Mother didn't seem to think she'd done anything wrong! She said you had to get what you could in this world!'

His eyes searched hers ruthlessly as he tried to assess her honesty. 'Sounds true to form. What else did she say?'

He leaned back slightly and she felt marginally less trapped. Emotion was almost choking her. She'd never known how materialistic her mother was.

She bit her lip, dismayed at how hopeless she was at judging people. All too often she'd taken them at face value, imagining that everyone was kind and well meaning. But that was naïve and unrealistic. Almost everyone was out for what they could get.

'We argued about what she'd done, but I could see I was getting nowhere. Then…I asked if Seamus was my father and she said…'

Lorcan was so tense he seemed like a coiled spring as he loomed over her. 'Yes?' he prompted in a dangerously low tone.

Kathleen gave an anguished shudder and swallowed back the thick constriction in her throat.

'She said she didn't know. He could be, so could one or two others!' she mumbled, pink with shame.

'Good grief!' Lorcan breathed.

Kathleen hung her head. 'She made it clear I'd always been a hindrance to her. I must have been blind not to realise I wasn't loved,' she mumbled.

He seemed about to say something and then changed his mind. 'What did you do?'

'I walked away and I've never seen her since.' She looked up anxiously. 'You do believe me, don't you?'

'I don't know what to say.' His brows were drawn hard over his eyes. 'I was so sure you knew about her affair with Father. I remember you said at the time that you understood why he'd warned me about you.'

'I did!' she said, puzzled. 'I thought he disapproved because my mother was just the housekeeper. She'd always told me that your family wouldn't approve of a friendship between you and me.'

'Oh, Kate!' he exclaimed in exasperation. 'It was nothing of the sort. Father was being cautious because of his own entanglement.'

She watched Lorcan's eyes close briefly in regret and she realised that they'd misunderstood one another with disastrous consequences.

'The awful thing is that because of all this Con has never seen his grandmother,' she mumbled. 'The only blood relative he's got apart from me.'

He studied her unhappy face with compassion. 'Perhaps it's just as well. Over the years she extracted money and gifts—some of them family jewellery—from my father. I think it was a case of ongoing blackmail. And several items of value went missing when she left.'

Kathleen gasped with horror. 'That's terrible! I'm sorry! I understand why you were so angry with me,' she said, stricken with shame. 'How could my mother have behaved like this? She's betrayed me. I loved her and she didn't care!' she finished jerkily.

He rested his hands on her drooping shoulders, stroking them in an attempt to calm her. 'Yes, that's natural. I do know how you feel,' he said in a low tone.

'No one knows!' she protested.

'I think I do. I lived in five children's homes and had nine sets of foster parents before I came here. I hated my birth mother for abandoning me and putting me through that. I'm not looking for pity, Kathleen,' he said quietly. 'I just want you to understand that I was rejected by my mother too.'

'But in your case she might have had a good reason for

not keeping you,' she pointed out. 'She might have been very young, or homeless, or without money—'

'I realised that, when I grew older,' he agreed evenly. 'And when I left here I decided to search for her and discover the truth.' His hands stilled. 'I wish I hadn't.'

'Was it awful?' she asked, horribly tempted to comfort him and soothe away the deep lines between his brows. 'I imagine it would have been a shock when you turned up—'

He gave a short, humourless laugh. 'It wasn't a shock. That would have suggested she had some emotional involvement in my existence. No. Her response was total indifference. I was *nothing* to her.' He took in a long and heavy breath, then let it out.

'How hard that must have been for you,' she said unhappily.

He smiled down at her. 'We're in the same boat, aren't we?' he said gently. 'It's the ultimate rejection. Mothers are supposed to love you unreservedly, to root for you when no one else cares. That's why I know it must have been extremely difficult for you to be suddenly alone at the age of seventeen. My heart goes out to you.'

He understood. She felt overwhelmed. 'Oh, Lorcan!' she choked, filling up.

He was very near to her but she could hardly see for the tears. When she blinked and cleared her vision a little, she saw that pain and sympathy had warmed and softened all the hard, uncompromising lines of his face. Instinctively she strained towards him, touched by his concern and wanting to soothe his own pain.

Slowly his head angled. His gaze dropped to her softly parted lips. In a daze, she watched the hard, grieving lines of his mouth become full and sensual. And as the distance between their mouths lessened imperceptibly, she realised with a start that he was about to kiss her.

'No! Not that!' she cried in panic.

With a swiftness that left him standing, she slid from his grasp and escaped into the conservatory, ignoring the ecstatic greeting from the dogs in her distress.

She'd been a fool. What must he think of her? That she was willing and available? That despite all her protestations she was as free with her favours as her mother? She groaned. The offer of a one-night-stand with Lorcan she did *not* need!

Worse still, the problem of the house still hadn't been solved. They had a long way to go, a lot of decisions to make before she could feel secure. She groaned. If he hadn't mistakenly branded her a tramp in the first place, they wouldn't be in this situation at all!

'Rot you, *rot* you, Lorcan FitzGerald!' she seethed, tears of shame and anger almost blinding her.

'Kathleen—'

'Go away! I've got work to do!' she jerked hysterically.

Ignoring him, she began sweeping the quarry-tiled floor vigorously as the tears spilled out unchecked. Lorcan was resurrecting things she'd rather forget.

Why didn't he leave her in peace? *Why* did he have to confront her with such painful events? And why had she suffered so much? *She* hadn't slept with Seamus, she thought crossly; it had been her mother. *She* hadn't come home drunk eight years ago; that had been Harry. And it was Lorcan, not she, who'd been the one who'd jumped to the wrong conclusion and blurted out a truth that should have stayed secret.

Yet it had all rebounded on *her*. Hating herself for wallowing in self-pity, she fought to control her sobs.

During Harry's worsening health and drunken rages, she'd soldiered on doggedly. There'd been no time to feel sorry for herself. But for some inexplicable reason her emotions had spilled out on seeing Lorcan. She knew she was close to breaking point and that made her furious. This was a time when she needed all her wits about her.

'Kathleen,' he murmured again.

Anger she could cope with. Gentleness and understanding were another matter entirely. She burst into tears and stood by an oleander tree howling, her whole body racked by misery.

Lorcan looked at her helplessly. His hastily reworked strategy had been to push her to the limit and beyond— and then go in for the kill, thus securing Ballykisteen when she was weak and vulnerable.

But as he came nearer to the tiny, pathetic figure that was almost swallowed up in the ludicrously over-large jumper, he knew she'd reached her limit already.

Instead of pressing home his advantage then, he did something extraordinary.

'Don't cry,' he said awkwardly.

'I'm *not*!' she sobbed, almost knocking over a small palm tree with her wild stabbing.

Touched by her stubborn refusal to acknowledge the obvious—that the tears had formed rivulets down her face— he found himself confronting her, one questing hand cupping her wet and tragic face.

'It must be raining salt water, then!' he suggested in gentle amusement.

Defeated, she dropped the broom and stared up at him mutely, huge tears forming in her sorrowful dark eyes. On an impulse, his arms went around her and she surrendered at once, her shoulders shaking convulsively as she sniffed pitifully into his fuchsia-pink shirt.

He felt a heel. And suddenly he had to tell her so. 'I'm really sorry,' he said contritely, his mouth murmuring against her silky hair. 'Forgive me for messing up your life. I'm shocked that you didn't know what your mother was up to. I would never have said anything if I'd realised, believe me.'

Her body was soft and pliable against his and he wanted to caress every inch. With difficulty he shut his mind to such delights and waited patiently. After a while her breathing became less erratic. By then, his was high in his throat.

He shut his eyes in pain. He'd been so jealous. The anguish of that moment when he'd seen her giggling as his hated brother pawed her was slicing through him even now. She'd bewitched him.

As she was close to bewitching him again. He put a slight space between their bodies before she realised what was happening to his libido.

But fatally she glanced up at him, her huge brown eyes swimming with tears, her lashes wet and giving her an appealingly forlorn appearance. And he took one look at her trembling mouth and, without knowing how it happened, he was kissing her lips gently, sipping the salt from them as if it was nectar.

He felt the quiver of her body, the answering pressure of her lush mouth, and he abandoned himself to the stolen moments of pleasure with the eagerness of a man long denied water.

CHAPTER SIX

His tenderness had melted all of Kathleen's defences. Desperate to prolong this moment, she slipped her hand around the warm smoothness of Lorcan's scalp and drew his head to her, increasing the fierce pressure on her mouth.

She wanted to be held like this for a long time, to feel the hardness of his body against hers, to know the reality of hugging someone who cared—however briefly.

His emotions were reeling; she knew that and it gave them a common bond. Maybe, she thought hazily, as their kisses became more and more passionate, they were both hungry for love and compassion.

Dimly she was aware that he was uttering little groans of desire. Instead of being afraid, she felt released, as if all responsibility had been taken from her.

'Hold me, Lorcan!' she whispered, taking his hands and leading them down to her hip. 'Hold me tightly! Touch me...'

'Kathleen!' he whispered harshly, and did so.

She let the warmth of his palms seep into her bones and luxuriated when they swept into the deep curve of her waist. For a moment his fingers nestled in the hollow there while his mouth parted hers and she pressed against him harder, knowing she was behaving badly but quite unable to stop herself.

Wonderingly she trailed her fingers over his face. And he shuddered, hauling her tightly to him, his mouth fiercely opening hers in a startling, profoundly erotic kiss that made her groan and grip his shoulders hard.

She wanted him. Badly. Instead of stopping his maraud-

78

ing hands, she encouraged their exploration, uttering little whimpers of ecstasy as he swept a tormenting finger across the mound of her firm breast.

And then from nowhere came a nasty little feeling that she was being driven by a desire she wouldn't be able to control. And therefore it was dangerous.

Lorcan sensed her brief distraction and pulled back, breathing heavily. But she took one look at the sculpted arch of his erotic mouth and groaned helplessly, reaching up to taste him again.

'No. This isn't a good idea,' he said thickly before their lips met.

They stood staring at each other, shaking with restrained passion. 'I know,' she said in a small, bewildered voice.

'Perhaps this will be the moment when we're interrupted by a telephone call. Or where the baby wakes,' he husked, his fingers snaking sensually over her hipbone as if he couldn't stop touching her.

They waited in silence, unable to tear their eyes from one another. Conor stubbornly slept on outside while heady perfumes from the exotic flowers in the conservatory tantalised their senses.

Lorcan's teeth grazed his lower lip. His gaze became dark and guarded as he disentangled himself from her.

'I don't want to get involved with you,' he said stiffly. 'It would be a disaster. You must see now that only one of us can live here.'

Why not both? she longed to cry. Seeing him again, touching him, had resurrected all her old passions. She ached for him so much that it scared her. She'd never felt so intense about anyone in the whole of her life—except her sons.

And yet she knew she didn't dare trust Lorcan if he had a tendency to get drunk. She wasn't going to put herself through that kind of relationship again.

Anger filled her. She wanted him and couldn't have him. Suddenly she wanted to kick something in frustration.

'I have prior claim. I've made my livelihood here,' she said roughly. 'Dec and I—'

'Ah, yes,' Lorcan said, icy and remote as if a switch had turned off inside him. 'I'd forgotten dear old Dec.'

She stiffened at his tone. 'For the last time,' she protested, 'we're not, and never have been, lovers!'

'So you say. Excuse me,' he said coldly.

'Where are you going?' she called in agitation to his retreating back. She wanted him to stay. To kiss her again, to make her forget the kind of man he was…

'To start sorting out Harry's desk,' he called without pausing.

She stared. 'But…we haven't come to any decision—'

He turned, his eyes flinty. 'I have. I'm staying,' he said tightly. 'You're going. You've got two days to pick up that cheque and find alternative accommodation. Don't cross me, Kathleen,' he warned. 'Or you'll regret it.'

Her body slumped. There was no point in running after him. He obviously regretted kissing her. It had been a moment of desperation for both of them. One of those awful mistakes.

She'd have to go. Lorcan would never share and he'd never let her be the sole mistress of Ballykisteen.

Depressed at her bleak prospects, she spent the rest of the day working like an automaton while Conor played happily beside her, unaware that their home was under threat. Her body felt empty, as if it had been promised much and given little. Lorcan had aroused her sexual appetite and left it dissatisfied.

Well, she'd just have to put it to sleep again!

That evening she put Con to bed, ignoring Lorcan, who'd spread piles of paper on the kitchen table, and ignoring too the cheque which he'd placed ostentatiously in the middle of the fruit bowl.

She didn't offer him any supper and after a while he went out—presumably to the pub. Perhaps a little maliciously, she didn't bother to make up a bed for him either and shut herself in her bedroom after supper. She wondered if he'd come knocking on her door and waited, her nerves making her jump at every sound.

When the front door slammed just after midnight, she held her breath in anticipation, her heartbeat thundering in her ears. He went into the kitchen and she heard him making a drink. She licked her parched lips and drew her dressing gown around her, her eyes huge in her anxious face.

And then he went away. Her mouth quivered. He was moving about upstairs. That was his door closing. Silence.

For no reason at all, she burst into tears.

'I saw that Lorcan's come back,' remarked Declan the next morning, when they began checking the orders in the kitchen. 'Didn't feel any earthquakes, though.'

'I did. Was he at the pub?' she muttered crossly, curious to know how he'd been received.

Declan nodded. 'He's got guts, I'll grant him that. You could have cut the silence with a butter knife but he sat there as large as life, greeting people and supping a pint and eating his stew as if we were all best friends. So…what's going to happen about the Manor?'

She told him how they'd reached a stalemate. 'He's very determined,' she said bitterly. 'I can understand why he wants to live here.'

'You stick up for yourself!' Dec reached out and gave her shoulders a squeeze. 'Village is all behind you.'

Kathleen felt a shiver go down her back. Half turning her head, she saw Lorcan standing in the doorway watching them, his face dark with contempt. Once again, her innocent and quite understandable affection for Dec had put her in a bad light!

Quickly she slipped from her friend's grasp and busied herself by pinning the order lists to the baskets, hating to be put in the same category as her mother. It made her feel cheap and nasty. Somehow she had to convince him of her innocence.

When she was picking roses in the garden later, she heard the sound of Lorcan's car going up the drive and turning onto the Ballykisteen road.

There was a note on the table when she went in for lunch. 'He's gone away for a few days, to see his mother in Dublin!' she cried in dismay.

Declan took the note and read it. 'That's good, isn't it?' he asked, puzzled.

Of course it was. She should be glad. Why then did she have such a feeling of loss? It was so stupid.

'It delays decisions,' she said by way of explanation. 'He's deliberately left me hanging around, like a—a—'

'Like a lovesick girl?' suggested Declan, washing his hands.

'What do you mean by that?' she demanded. 'If you think for one minute—!' He turned in surprise and she realised she was overreacting. 'Sorry,' she said with a forced laugh. 'I'm ratty. I want the whole thing sorted. Now.'

'I suppose Mrs FitzGerald will come back with him,' Dec mused.

Kathleen felt a rush of horror sweep through her. 'Of course!' She groaned. 'That's me finished for sure,' she said gloomily. 'She'd never co-exist with me. I'd remind her of my mother too much.'

Declan said nothing, but he came over and gave her one of his bear hugs. 'Come and live with Bridget and me,' he said generously. 'You can expand the cookery side of the business—'

'Thanks,' she muttered, all the fight gone out of her.

And she spent the rest of the week mooning over the Manor, looking at its elegant rooms and beautiful gardens with a new intensity, so that she could absorb every detail and store them in her memory for ever.

Any day now Lorcan and his mother would return. Although this would bring problems for her, she longed to see him. Every time she thought of him her heart started pumping furiously as she remembered the feel of his lips on hers, the wonderful feeling when he'd held her in his arms.

But that wouldn't happen again. Her mouth drooped and then she pulled herself together, packing her van with deliveries. It looked as if she'd have to accept the situation. It wouldn't be too bad, she reasoned. She and Con would live in the village and make a new life for themselves. But it would be awful with Lorcan and his mother looking down their noses at her whenever they crossed her path.

Kathleen clenched her teeth. She didn't want to go! Hated the idea of Lorcan winning! Angrily she flung herself into the van and switched on the ignition. Nothing happened.

'Blow! Wretched starter motor again!' she complained.

Muttering under her breath, she grabbed a spanner and dived out to fiddle under the bonnet.

Once again, she thought crossly, she was paying dearly for a situation someone else had created. If Harry hadn't been so vindictive as to leave half the estate to Lorcan—

'Oh, *no!*' she wailed, when the spanner slipped from her fingers.

She crouched down and peered under the van. Grumbling, she lay on the ground and eased herself beneath the engine. At that moment, she heard a car approaching.

She groaned. It was almost certainly Lorcan and his

mother. Just her luck to be hot and bothered and crawling in the dirt!

There came the clunk of a door and the progress of leather-shod feet across the drive. Two well-polished brown shoes gleamed at her.

'Still here, then,' came Lorcan's annoyed voice.

Furious with the injustice of her situation, she grabbed the spanner just as a dollop of oil splashed on her face.

'Ooof!' Spluttering, she slid out from beneath the troublesome van.

'Doesn't look good,' observed Lorcan.

Scrubbing an old rag over her face, she thought, No, but he did. Casual peacock-blue shirt, oatmeal trousers and jacket. And there was a sultriness about his mouth and eyes that caused her hands to shake.

Panic-stricken, she plucked up courage to glance at his car. No mother! Her hopes rose.

'Are you talking about me or the van?' she asked, determined to appear jaunty.

'You look your usual self,' he drawled.

'Oh.' Great compliment. Her 'usual' was apparently dirty, flustered and grungy! Crushed, she tried the ignition again. Nothing happened. 'Help me rock it, will you?' she asked irascibly, spreading her hands on the side of the van.

'What's wrong?' he asked when she'd tried the ignition again.

Kathleen was ready to throw things. 'I don't know! It's usually the starter motor but not this time,' she said grumpily, already worrying about the repair costs.

'Put it on the scrap heap,' Lorcan advised drily, and went to open the boot of his car.

Kathleen suddenly needed to know what was happening. 'How…how's your mother?' She flushed, embarrassed by the unnatural pitch of her voice.

'Delirious.'

Her eyes darkened with anxiety. What did that mean? 'I'm glad for you both. Coming back, is she?'

He slammed the boot lid down and looked at her thoughtfully. 'No. She has a full and eventful life in Dublin. When I offered to bring her back, she refused point-blank—but ordered me to visit her often.'

Kathleen could have wept with relief. There was hope for her yet. 'Did you tell her about me?'

'I did.' A faint smile played about his mouth. 'She warned me to be careful.' He came over to her and dabbed at her chin with his handkerchief while she held her breath. 'I told her I could handle you.'

Her eyes flashed angrily. Arrogant brute! 'Well, handle this. I need help,' she said bluntly, eyeing his car with covetous intent. 'I've got deliveries to make. Can I borrow your car?'

'Certainly not!'

He turned and walked towards the house. Kathleen hastily planted herself in his path, her hair flying loose about her face as she confronted him.

'Don't take out your dislike of me on my customers. Their businesses rely on me. If I let them down it'll be all over the county. And I'll make sure people get to know the reason!' she threatened hotly.

He frowned and studied her for a moment, his face a blank. 'All right. But I'm driving. Give me a moment to sort myself out and I'll take you wherever you want to go—providing everyone gets to know what a good Samaritan I've been.'

'OK! Bargain! Thank you!' she cried in delight. 'I'll load up. I'm delivering to Louisburgh and Delphi Lodge if that's all right.'

He stiffened. 'Up the Famine Road?' A frown pulled his brows together. 'Just my luck,' he muttered. Pausing beneath the portico, he looked back at her. 'Where's Conor? Has he been abducted and sold to slavers?'

She went pale at his version of an old joke they'd shared as teenagers and automatically grabbed her locket, but she quickly recovered and even managed a laugh.

'He's in Bridget's nursery school. Whenever I've got a lot of work on, he totters off with her and has a lovely time.' She wiped her hot brow. 'He loves it so much that it makes me feel redundant!'

'You must be grateful to her for being so generous. I'm damned if I'd take my lover's bastard,' he said frostily, and went inside.

Kathleen heaved in a huge breath. Until she convinced him that her relationship with Declan was innocent, he'd continue to treat her like dirt. Vowing to put him straight, she hurried indoors to clean herself up.

That day, Connemara was at its most beautiful. The softly rounded mountains rose like fat green buns into the cloudless sky. Sheep and cattle wandered across the roads, grazing on the rich green peatlands on either side and forcing Lorcan to adopt a leisurely pace.

Kathleen didn't mind. She usually took her time on this delivery run anyway. They'd both wound their windows down and were enjoying the crystal fresh air. Several times Lorcan stopped the car by one of the hundreds of loughs and stood silently on a sandy shoreline, surveying the peaceful scene.

The further they progressed, the more she could see how deeply he loved his homeland. There was a soft smile on his face permanently now, a lightness to his step as he walked back to the car.

At Louisburgh she made her deliveries, helped willingly by Lorcan. 'Just the Delphi Lodge drop now,' she announced as they drove off again. 'I—I'd like to stop there for a short walk. You don't have to come. I always do it when I'm on this trip—'

'I know. I will too,' he said softly.

Her heart bumped up and down as she stared into his soft green eyes. 'Good,' she said, as naturally as her dry throat would allow her.

Perhaps, she thought, they could come to an amicable arrangement. He seemed different. Warmer, happier.

After the delivery he parked the car further down the Famine Road by a standing stone. She wondered if he was aware that he'd chosen this spot before, when he'd come back from university. But she said nothing. It was long ago, shortly before he'd broken her heart.

They began to walk. River torrents streamed down the steep mountain in silver cascades and there was the heady coconut smell of furze drifting on the breeze. It was a romantic spot, nestling among the mountains with the lapping waters of Doo Lough making it one of the most peaceful scenes in the world. And the site of a tragedy.

Lorcan remembered every moment of the last time they'd walked the Famine Road. He'd been touched by Kathleen's passionate involvement with people she'd never known. She'd aroused his protective instincts and put him in touch with his emotions.

Even today her face was reflecting her thoughts and he wanted to put his arm around her to whisper that it was all right, she needn't be sad, it was all a long time ago. And then he remembered Declan, and the urge disappeared in a fog of anger.

The road ran the eleven miles from Louisburgh to the large, peat-dark lake where Delphi Lodge stood. During the famine in the mid-nineteenth century the hunting lodge had been the destination of the starving inhabitants of Louisburgh. Men, women and children had walked the eleven miles in a raging blizzard to collect letters of permission from officials at the lodge, so that they could be fed and housed in the Poor House.

The officials had been far too busy eating dinner, however, and had told the people to apply in the morning. But few of the four hundred who'd set out had remained alive by then. Most, weakened by despair, starvation and the cruel night, had frozen to death.

He knew that Kathleen always liked to walk a little of the road when she could, and to remember those poor souls who'd perished. He steeled himself against the inevitable as she paused by the lake, bowed her head and said a prayer.

But he too found himself moved by the thought of the people's plight and the cruelty of the men who'd been warm and sheltered and too engrossed in their own pleasures to bother about the homeless.

He cared passionately about injustices, especially those which left people without food and shelter. This poignant spot had always touched his heart too. Once again the emotion it evoked was softening his resolve to remain aloof and distant from Kathleen.

Today, she seemed particularly upset. As he watched her, standing still and silent a few feet away, small silver tears began to seep from her eyes.

He wondered if she was thinking of her own plight, when she and her mother had been turned out. It had been a hard action on his mother's part—but understandable in the circumstances.

Kathleen lifted her head and met his troubled eyes.

'It was a terrible thing that happened,' she said with a sniff.

'Terrible.' He cleared his throat, annoyed that he'd been hi-jacked by emotion too. 'Don't upset yourself.'

She managed a brave smile. 'I know, I'm soft. My

mother was always appalled by what she called my water-works!'

Somehow he stopped himself from gathering her in his arms even though she looked more beautiful and forlorn than he'd ever known. Her gypsy curls were dancing on her forehead and her eyes were black and bright with tears. A tear or two had reached the groove above her mouth and he ached to kiss it dry. And take her mouth in his...

He swallowed, seeing she was waiting for a comment. 'Caring about other people isn't soft,' he said gruffly.

If only he would hold her, she thought wistfully. She felt very alone. But he was determined to keep his distance. Almost certainly his mother had added to his low opinion of her during his recent visit.

'Let's go back,' she said dejectedly.

Lorcan didn't know if he was glad or sorry that the walk had been uneventful. Back in the car he fell silent, seeing for the first time how his future stretched ahead in all its dull predictability: Ballykisteen, visits to his mother, his work.

His glance slid to Kathleen, her small face absorbed and thoughtful as she watched the passing scenery, every inch of her body tense with the passion she felt for her country.

He envied the freedom with which she expressed emotion. But she spread her love around too generously. And revealing passion and emotion only opened you up to being kicked in the teeth.

He didn't want that. So what was left? A well-ordered life, safe from hurt...which suddenly wasn't enough.

He sighed. Kathleen, for all the dangers she presented, was becoming an obsession with him. His body and mind were filled with her and when she was near it took all his will-power not to grab her like some sex-starved adolescent. Inexplicable.

Irritably he scowled at the narrow road ahead, noticing

idly a mob of hooded crows circling in the sky. Then they swooped on something on the tarmac. As he drove towards them he suddenly flung his arm protectively across Kathleen and braked violently.

'Sorry! Hold on a minute!' he called, already leaping from the car.

The crows rose in a heavy flapping of wings as he approached and he crouched down to see what they'd been after. It was a miserable-looking wagtail. Gently he picked it up, bringing it back in his cupped hands.

'What is it?' she asked curiously, when he slid in beside her again.

He showed her, transferring it gently to her lap. They both studied the bedraggled little bird anxiously. 'I think its wing's broken, poor little thing.'

'I'll take care of it.' She looked up in admiration. 'Most men would have driven on.'

Stupidly, he felt as pleased as if he'd won a coveted prize. 'I couldn't,' he muttered.

Their gazes locked. 'You're soft too,' she said quietly, her eyes huge and dark, swallowing him in their liquid depths. 'You have a heart. Why are you so determined to hide it?'

And to his surprise, she reached out and pulled his head down till her soft, warm lips met his.

'Let's get this little bird somewhere warm and safe,' she said shakily, her words whispering softly against his mouth. 'And then we must talk.'

He made a hash of finding the right gear. His brain seemed to have stuck in neutral. He wanted her desperately. Declan received her favours, why not him? A battle went on between his head and his loins. Given the right circumstances, he was sure she'd let him make love to her. But...

He raked his hand through his hair impatiently, unable

to understand why his conscience kept telling him to leave
her alone. Why should he? Others hadn't been so inhibited.

Hot and aching, he fought for detachment. It was wrong,
wrong. Kathleen had inadvertently learnt immorality from
her mother's womb. At least, he thought, surreptitiously
watching her rapt face as she peeped at the bird, she had
the excuse of uncontrollable passions, whereas her mother
had been purely mercenary.

It didn't mean, though, that he was free to take advantage
of her willingness. Except, his baser instincts argued slyly,
he'd be taking her from Declan! What a noble guy he was
to act selflessly on Bridget's behalf, he thought drily, fully
aware that he'd been searching for any excuse to satisfy
his primal needs.

Sitting beside him, Kathleen felt the quiet joy steal over
her. She knew Lorcan had opened up a little more than
he'd intended, and was disturbed by his emotions. Good!

Thrilled with the change in her prospects for the future,
she had no hesitation in sending Lorcan into the nursery
school for Conor and her heart turned over when he appeared with the little boy perched excitedly on his shoulders.

Con's fat hands were gripping Lorcan's short blond hair
fiercely but Lorcan was grinning and his face seemed
flushed as if they'd been playing an energetic game.

'Will you give Con his tea?' she asked innocently, when
Lorcan had carried Con into the house. 'I'll see to the wagtail.'

Lorcan looked panic-stricken. 'Can't one of them wait?'

She laughed. 'Babies and animals want their needs satisfied *now*!' He gave her a smouldering glance from under
his lashes and she drew in a breath, her stomach clenching
with her own clamouring needs. 'I'll direct you,' she promised, faltering when he continued to fell her with his
sexy look.

Stumbling over her words as she told Lorcan what to do with Con, she got them both settled, her face soft and wistful as Lorcan fed her son with gentle care and she set the bird's wing as the vet had taught her.

Were her instincts right about Lorcan? she wondered, popping the little wagtail in a dark box to recover. Could she find the key to unlock his good nature and work out a way for them to split the estate fairly? She felt excited. Her eyes sparkled with hope.

But first, she had to deal with the outstanding orders. 'If you'll be all right for a moment,' she said happily, 'I'll just check the answer-machine and pop down to Declan's with the lists. He's doing the deliveries tomorrow.' She beamed at Lorcan, eagerly anticipating the ending of their feud.

He scanned her animated face and his eyes narrowed. 'Where's Bridget?' he asked sharply.

Kathleen blinked. 'I don't know! Why? She might be still at the nursery if—'

'*I'll* take the lists to Declan's.'

Interpreting the taut subtext behind his offer, she glared at him in exasperation. 'I'm not sneaking off for a quick cuddle, if that's what you're thinking!'

'Prove it.'

'How?' She could explain about Dec and tell him she was innocent till she was puce but he'd never listen. What it needed was evidence…

She drew in a sharp breath. Her eyes lit up. Immediately, Lorcan glanced at her suspiciously, as if she were about to slip a knife into his ribs.

'You don't trust me at all, do you?' she said wryly.

'Have I any reason to?'

'What happened to the rule of law here that people are innocent till proven guilty?' she shot.

'It's obvious that you manipulated Harry into marriage— presumably with a wiggle or two and a few sultry glances,' he said coldly. 'And I'm convinced you carried on an affair with Declan during your marriage, that child being the result. I could get a conviction on the evidence I have.'

'Then be prepared for the defence's surprise evidence, Mr Prosecutor,' she said haughtily. 'I'll leave the lists for now since they bother you so much. I can hand them over later. Shall we go into the drawing room?'

Lorcan shrugged as if he didn't care what they did and picked up a folder from Harry's desk. Smugly, Kathleen cleaned up Conor, slid him to her hip and, grabbing a handful of toys, followed Lorcan across the hall into the beautifully proportioned room.

He made himself comfortable on the damask-covered chesterfield and opened the folder, busying himself with its contents. She felt almost as though they were a family and her heart somersaulted at the thought.

It could be like that. Not family, perhaps, but friendship. Even as those words came into her head, she knew she was lying to herself. She did want more. And being out on the Famine Road had somehow reminded Lorcan of the affection they'd once shared. Anything was possible.

So she *had* to win him over. Breathing quickly, she knelt on the antique Persian carpet, settled her son with his xylophone and sat back on her heels, looking around her in a daze of optimistic delight.

'Assessing the value of each item?' Lorcan asked sarcastically.

She refused to be put off by the fact that he didn't trust her. He'd had a lifetime of being let down. Soon he'd learn that she could be relied on. Pleased with that prospect, she smiled.

'I wouldn't have a clue,' she said with a laugh. 'Only that everything seems so right in this room. It's just perfect. Would you make the fire?'

He hesitated, then assembled the paper, kindling and turf

which she kept in the copper tub. In a few moments the
fire was blazing away, giving out its wonderful peaty
aroma. Lorcan fixed the fireguard in place and Kathleen
was touched that he'd been thinking of Con's safety.

Conor toddled over to Lorcan where he knelt on the rug
and gripped his arm, looking up at his rapt face solemnly.
As if he hardly knew what he was doing, Lorcan absently
stroked Con's dark head and the little boy clambered onto
his lap while Kathleen held her breath. The two of them
sat like that for a while, watching the leaping flames. A
lump came to her throat.

If only, she thought. If only.

'I'd like to change out of these clothes and into something tidier,' she said quietly. 'Can you hold the fort with
Con for a short time? I want to invite Dec and his family
over here for an hour or so.'

His head jerked around as if she'd suddenly whipped
him. 'Put on your glad rags for him if you must, but I have
a pressing engagement elsewhere,' he said, tight-lipped.

'Please stay, Lorcan,' she said softly. 'You asked for
proof and I'm going to provide it. I want to show you how
much Declan loves Bridget.'

'The mind boggles,' he scathed, abandoning Conor and
returning grim-faced to the sofa.

Nursing a humiliating pang of jealousy, he watched
Kathleen as she walked eagerly to the phone. She'd become
excited at the thought of seeing her boyfriend. Her face had
come alive. What chance did he have in the face of such
love?

His brow furrowed as he forced himself to focus on the
bills he was supposed to be paying, but he was too interested in the conversation she was now having.

'Dec! It's me, Kate!' she said enthusiastically.

Irritably Lorcan ripped up the cheque he'd just spoiled.
He'd never heard anyone so eager and breathless.

Apparently her lover was pleased at the prospect of seeing her—even with someone else around—because she cheerfully said, 'Goodbye, see you soon,' and replaced the receiver.

'I won't be long!' she said, her eyes bright with happiness.

There wasn't anything he could say. His throat was clogged up with anger. When she began to sing as she ran off to change, Lorcan had to grit his teeth to stop himself from going after her and saying exactly what he thought of women who encouraged men to cheat on their wives.

He'd leave that till later. First, he'd warn Declan off. If he didn't sock him on the jaw for starters instead. Hell. The muscles in his stomach were murdering his digestion again.

The child put its hands on his knees, looking up at him with Kathleen's dark, melting eyes. Like her, the kiddie was irresistible. Since she wasn't there to see him, he pushed aside the papers and got down on the floor, letting Con clamber all over him.

Flushed and happy, wearing a honey-gold, full-skirted dress, Kathleen tiptoed to the drawing room door, alerted by the sounds of giggling and peculiar noises.

To her delight, Lorcan was putting Con through his paces. First he folded his arms and Con copied as best he could. Then he pointed, then waved, bowed, did a jig…

He was laughing at Con's sweet attempts to mimic his actions and he seemed almost unrecognisable. Kathleen adored him then, falling instantly in love with the hidden, secret man who had been locked up behind a wall of distrust.

Moist-eyed, she leaned against the doorjamb, drinking in his beauty and the suppleness of his body as he swept Con into the air and then down to the ground. Against his shirt, the muscles of his arms and torso strained and relaxed. The familiar liquid warmth flooded into her veins and she wondered nervously whether she was wise to take the course she'd planned.

Perhaps it was madness to believe they could live in the same house. She was too ready to surrender and he could hurt her.

Wide-eyed, she watched as Lorcan caught her son to him and held him close in exactly the same the way she did, adoring the feel of Con's firm little body, smelling his baby smell, brushing the peachy cheek with his lips. It was the most telling behaviour and touched her heart to the core.

A whisper of sweet pain must have escaped her because he looked up then and immediately moved back from Con. 'You're back. You can amuse your own child now,' he said flatly, resuming his seat.

But he shot her a second glance, his eyes warming as they looked her up and down, dwelling for heart-stopping moments on her bare throat, the low neckline and every emphasised curve of her body on the way down.

Simmering with an extraordinary mixture of emotions, she sank gracefully to the floor. 'Yes, Lorcan,' she said meekly, sitting by Con's hammer and peg set and giving it a few taps to attract her son's attention.

'Do you entertain Declan here often?' Lorcan asked in a husky growl.

'Only with Bridget and the children,' she replied evenly, despite the fact that his gaze seemed to keep returning to examine her body. She tucked her legs under her skirts. 'I wish you'd use that clever, legal brain of yours,' she said with a sigh. 'Would someone who loathed her own mother's part in adultery be involved in adultery herself?'

He grunted, his eyes brooding as he returned her level gaze. 'People aren't always consistent. They're very quick to condemn others for faults they exhibit themselves.'

For a moment she wished he'd been something less adversarial, like a painter of kittens on chocolate boxes.

'I bet you're a wow in court,' she sighed.

'Don't miss a trick. I warn you, Kate, if you flirt with Declan or use this opportunity—'

'I won't. I never have. You'll learn why. Trust me.'

His mouth became bitter. 'Never,' he muttered as the doorbell went.

In a smooth, fluid movement, she rose to her feet, aware that every inch of her body was being explored again by Lorcan's hot gaze.

Drawing herself up to her full height, she said with quiet confidence, 'You will, oh, you will, Lorcan!'

A slow smile spread across her face as she imagined the change in their relationship when he understood her and shed his suspicions.

As if driven by some uncontrollable force, he reached out his hand and pulled her towards him, looking up at her with an unreadable expression. Suddenly he stood up and took her face between his hands, kissing her with unexpected force.

The bell rang again. A frantic craving rose in her and she wanted to ignore it. But he abandoned her as quickly as he'd claimed her and she stumbled blindly to the door, trying to push air into her gasping lungs.

'Wow! You look S-E-X-Y!' exclaimed Bridget, spelling the word because of four-year-old Maire, who'd flung her arms around Kathleen's legs in greeting.

'What's the invite for, me darlin'?' whispered Declan, clutching a small bag of toys. 'If you're trying to vamp Lorcan in that dress and get him to give in to your every wish, you'll do better on your own without a pack of gooseberries watching!'

Flustered, she picked up Maire. 'I thought I'd give you the order list and introduce you to Lorcan properly,' she said in embarrassment.

'Oh, right. Well, we won't stay long,' Bridget said, amused.

'What's that meant to imply?' Kathleen asked uncertainly.

Her friend put her arm around her shoulders. 'It means I know perfectly well why your face is flushed and why your eyes are shining.'

'Why's that?' asked Declan, mystified.

Bridget raised her eyes to heaven. 'Men!' she said with a grin. 'Why are they always the last to know?'

'Know what?' complained Declan as they came to the drawing room.

Bridget leaned close and whispered in his ear. 'Kate's got the hots for Lorcan!'

Yes, she had, Kathleen thought—and immediately came face to face with Lorcan himself. Had he heard? There was only polite interest in his expression, though she noticed he was breathing heavily.

Horribly compromised, she waited for them all to make their wary greetings then took the chance to escape for a moment and fetch drinks for the children.

When she returned, her face set in neutral again, Lorcan was asking courteous questions about the nursery and the children. He didn't speak to Declan at all.

Kathleen perched on the end of the chesterfield, her knees weak with nerves as Lorcan fended off questions about himself and conversation consequently became awkward.

'Dec, how about reading Maire's favourite story?' she said in desperation.

'Not here,' he protested. 'People wouldn't want—'

'Please,' broke in Lorcan unexpectedly. 'Read to your child.'

There was a little hush. 'Go on,' pleaded Kathleen, knowing this might sway Lorcan's opinion.

'OK.' Amiably, Declan sat on the chaise longue with the fairy story in his huge hands.

At once, Maire, Bridget and baby Finn arranged themselves on the floor in front of him, eyeing him with their usual adoration as he began to read. Anyone could see that this was a ritual, practised often and much enjoyed.

With Conor half-asleep in her arms, Kathleen slid to the seat of the sofa and relaxed. This was what she'd wanted Lorcan to see.

As he read, Declan acted out the parts with heart-wrenching intensity—the roaring, gesticulating giant, the tinkly-voiced princess and the brave prince. Every now and then he paused to stroke Bridget's hair or plant a kiss on an uplifted face at random—gestures so natural and instinctive that anyone could see they were prompted by a deep and abiding love.

Kathleen beamed. Dear Dec. No one could possibly have any doubt that he was a devoted husband and father.

And yet her affection was tinged with sorrow. She'd wanted a family like this all her life. Moist-eyed, she flicked a quick glance at Lorcan, to see if he'd noticed her give-away emotions.

And was stunned.

He looked shattered. No, *anguished.*

'Lorcan!' she whispered in concern.

He started, and his expression changed so quickly to detached disinterest that she thought she must have been hallucinating. From that moment on he said nothing other than the occasional monosyllable for the remainder of the O'Flahertys' visit.

And when they had left by the back way, he walked swiftly back into the hall and out of the front door without saying a word.

She was utterly dismayed. Her plan had backfired.

'Wretched man!' she muttered, almost tempted to stamp

her foot in frustration. 'You're the most stubborn person I've ever known!'

Why wouldn't he relent? He ought to be apologising to her and admitting that she was just an ordinary, decent human being and not some vamp straight off the pages of a tabloid newspaper!

And then she'd smile and he'd thaw a little and later they'd kiss…

No more of that! she told herself ruthlessly. The torture was unbearable. But she knew her body would continue to make its demands and her heart would ache with longing because of her firm belief that she and Lorcan could be soulmates.

'Give him time,' she whispered. 'One day he'll realise.'

After Conor's bath and three ritual readings of *The Naughty Pig*, with much lifting of flaps in the book to find where Naughty Pig was hiding, she tucked her son up in bed then started to prepare dinner.

Her heart thudded at every sound and she kept rushing to the window, thinking Lorcan might be coming up the drive. When he didn't, she felt increasingly nervous, like a girl on her first date.

And, she thought ruefully, catching a glimpse of herself in the mirror over the mantelpiece, she gave every impression of being one. It had been a long time since she'd worn a dress and she didn't want to dwell too long on why she'd chosen to do so.

Except, she told herself defensively, that she'd reckoned it wouldn't do her cause any harm if she looked nice. Nice! Her guilty glance slanted to the mirror again. Her hair was loose so that it flowed around her face and shoulders like a rippling black river. It was erotic and sexy, not nice, hence Bridget's surprised remark.

If it had been obvious to her friend, how had it looked

to Lorcan? She bit her lip. Perhaps that was why he'd escaped—he'd feared she intended to get her claws into him.

Restlessly she checked her watch. The pub had closed ages ago. It was getting late. She looked out into the night, wondering where he was. But he was an adult and responsible for himself and she had Con to think of. She could hardly go searching for him like an anxious parent...

And then she drew in a quick breath. Once before when he'd been distraught, Lorcan had vanished all night.

Had he compared Dec's idyllic family with his own? Had he remembered the last terrible time eight years ago when the FitzGeralds had all been together?

Her mind flashed back, running through the events.

Lorcan had just announced that his father had been committing adultery for the past eighteen years. Mrs FitzGerald had rushed off in hysterics to confront the unsuspecting Seamus in the study.

Lorcan had stood in the hall watching his parents arguing. His face had been as white as a sheet as the row intensified. Suddenly he'd grabbed a waxed jacket and marched out into the stormy winter night.

Still in her nightdress, Kathleen had run to the door and called for him to come back, but he'd ignored her. In seconds she'd been soaked from the torrential rain and she'd given up, certain that he'd be forced back by the terrible weather.

An hour before dawn he had still been missing. She and her mother, unable to sleep, had been packing their things in stony enmity, the gale howling around the house like a banshee.

They'd heard the sound of men's voices in the kitchen next door and it had become clear that Seamus had set up a search party for Lorcan. Seamus had sounded exhausted, as if he'd been up all night too.

Perhaps distress and tiredness had made Seamus careless

during the search, or maybe he'd been caught by a sudden gust of wind or a large wave. Whatever the cause, she'd learnt later that Lorcan had been discovered on Lettereen Point, cradling his father's dead body.

As she recalled the tragedy, her face paled. It had been hard for her to leave without seeing Lorcan again.

Harry had told her later that there were many who believed that Lorcan had pushed his father off the rocks during a heated argument, thus causing his death. Spiteful gossip had virtually driven Lorcan away.

Kathleen tried to imagine Lorcan's feelings at that time. He'd always seemed self-sufficient and invulnerable, but now she knew better. It must have broken his heart to leave his mother, his home, and the place where his father was buried. No wonder he was determined to stay.

Afraid for the future, she tidied up, then climbed the stairs and made up the bed in the master suite for him. If he did return late, he could sleep in comfort.

Her fingers stilled in the middle of plumping a pillow. Perhaps he'd gone out to get drunk, drowning his sorrows just like Harry. She shuddered in disgust and fear, turned too quickly and brought a pile of videos on a small table crashing to the floor.

She bent to pick them up, her hands trembling with distress as she relived the memories of life with Harry. The last thing she wanted was to be shouted at again.

She had no stomach for cleaning up after a drunken Lorcan, however sexy and desirable he might be when sober.

Sick with nerves, she smoothed out the duvet and decided to lock Con and herself in her bedroom for safety. Her gaze fell on the videos and it occurred to her that one or two of those might pass the time and take her mind off things.

Downstairs, she secured the door with trembling fingers,

made a cup of cocoa to comfort herself and settled down to watch the first video, entitled—intriguingly—*Hearts and Minds 4*.

And got a shock.

CHAPTER SEVEN

LORCAN was feeling chilled, despite some energetic walking and thinking over the past few hours, during which he'd reshaped his future to his total satisfaction.

As he came cheerfully into the walled garden he could see a light on in the housekeeper's room. Its warm glow instantly attracted him. The moon was bright, illuminating the garden beautifully, but it was a cold and ghostly silver not the cosy, welcoming flicker of a turf fire.

He needed warmth. Company, too. Seeing Declan's happiness had hurt more than he could have imagined possible. And he'd decided to do something about that.

Passing near the window, he couldn't resist glancing in on Kathleen. She was curled up on a sofa with two scraggy cats-in-need on her lap and a mug of something beside her. She was completely absorbed in some television programme, her face lovely in its delight.

Unobserved, he came closer, unable to resist a longer look. There was something rather underhand about what he was doing but the compulsion was greater than his conscience.

Light glimmered on her rippling cavalier curls, which cascaded enticingly about her small, rapt face. The close-fitting gold-coloured dress caressed her body with an enviable intimacy. Her fingers toyed with the silver locket she always wore, drawing his gaze to her breasts, which pressed against the fabric of her dress so forcefully as she leaned forwards that he could trace their firm, high outline in exciting detail.

He closed his eyes for a moment, overcome by the activity in his sex-starved body. She could dry his throat with a smile. What she was doing to him as she wriggled and stretched her sublime body on that sofa was quite extraordinary.

Her shoes lay discarded on the floor. Avidly he let his gaze drift, starting with her tiny pink toes…

He clenched his jaw, shaken by the image of himself on his knees, pressing his lips to the shapely hollows of her high-arched feet.

Or her smooth, gleaming legs. Thighs concealed by the billowing skirt, but slender. Tiny waist, as he knew, heaven to his searching hands…

Lorcan groaned. He couldn't go on like this! He wanted her. Time to move in on her. She wanted him; he wanted her. No problem.

But he found himself frowning and strangely reluctant to sweep in with a killing line in seductive sweet nothings. There was a touching artlessness and purity in her face which made him want to protect her from harm, not take advantage.

Was he a fool, or what? Granted she'd been innocent of conspiracy with her mother, and now he knew that she was innocent too of any sexual involvement with Declan.

But that didn't change the fact that she'd pursued her ambitions through Harry, selling herself like some cheap tart. If he was to keep his emotions intact, he'd be wise to remember that.

He looked down at the three-legged cat which was rubbing itself against his legs. He smiled wryly. A typical waif and stray of Kathleen's! As he bent to stroke its tortoise-shell-coloured head, he conceded that Kathleen's ambition to better herself would work in his favour. He'd get what he wanted with the minimum of trouble.

The house and children. With the prospect of great sex thrown in. She'd get the same.

The cat purred loudly, delirious with pleasure. How easy it was to satisfy animal instincts for food, shelter and attention! With a grin, he scooped up the cat and straightened, his fingers gently massaging its silky soft head.

Intriguingly, he could see that Kathleen was laughing. He craned his neck to the side so that he could see which programme she found so amusing.

His eyes widened. It was one of his.

It seemed as though a weight had fallen from his shoulders. Kathleen's hostility couldn't survive that!

His heart beat loudly as he let himself into the kitchen and deposited the cat on a chair. He mustn't rush this.

Suddenly aware of a wonderful aroma coming from the oven, he investigated its contents, carefully removed a huge pie and cut himself a generous portion, his hands shaking with excitement.

There was the sound of a bolt being drawn and Kathleen's glossy head poked cautiously around the door. It took all his self-control to conceal his extreme tension.

'Hope you don't mind,' he said, gesturing to the pie and popping another forkful of chicken and mushroom into his mouth.

She eyed him as if he might leap up and bite her too.

'I left it for you.'

He gave a small frown. Because of the video, he'd expected her to be friendly, but she was keeping the door between them both.

'Do you think I'm going to leap up and ravish you when there's chicken pie to be eaten?' he asked drily.

She blushed and answered with typical honesty, 'I was...afraid of you.'

He flinched. 'Afraid?' he asked in horror, adding quickly. 'I wouldn't harm a hair of your head, Kathleen.'

'Well, I thought you'd been out drinking,' she explained, still wary.

He relaxed. She was scared of memories, not him. He wondered what it had been like, married to Harry, and he felt the anger filling his guts with bile. Kathleen shrank back and he checked his rage quickly.

'Don't be frightened,' he soothed. 'I'm angry with Harry, not you. I can imagine that you went through a hard time with him.'

His mouth tightened at the misery in her eyes. Somehow he held himself in check, though every muscle in his body was urging him to let off a string of invective against his bullying brother and rush over to console the unhappy, trembling Kathleen.

'It's why I run a mile from drunks, even happy, merry ones. I can't help it but it isn't something I can control,' she said in a small voice.

'Not one drop of alcohol has passed my lips, I swear.'

'Oh.'

He saw that she was still uncertain, her eyes huge with anxiety, and he felt appalled that Harry had left her with such a legacy. The urge to comfort her was overwhelming. He made do with a warm smile.

'My turn for proof, then,' he said lightly. 'What shall it be? Shall I walk a chalk line, recite Volume One on the *Principles and Practices of International Law, Children's Section*, or Peter Piper picked a peck of pickled pepper?'

She gave a little nervous laugh and the hope in her eyes told him that she dearly wanted to believe what he was saying.

'I couldn't even manage that sentence sober,' she admitted.

He laughed. 'So I'm not drunk? I'll breathe on you if you like.'

'No!' she croaked. He watched her clear her throat and all he could think of was that his mouth could be there, tasting her silken skin… 'I reckon you're an alcohol-free zone,' she said breathily.

'I'm relieved. Does that mean I can talk to you without a six-foot slab of solid pine between us?'

'Oh! Yes!'

Almost shyly, she emerged into the kitchen. Lorcan felt the muscles in his body screw into tight knots when she came into full view. It was nigh impossible to stay in his seat. If the tortoiseshell cat hadn't leapt onto his lap, he might have given in to all his urges and grabbed her. But he stroked the cat instead. It wasn't much of a substitute, however.

'One of your projects?' he asked, nodding at the cat and congratulating himself on his almost neutral voice.

'Yes, poor darling!' She took a step as if intending to stroke it and he tensed. To his relief, Kathleen stopped, her hands fidgeting in front of her. 'She was horribly battered when I rescued her,' she said brightly. 'She doesn't like people much. I've no idea why she's befriended you.'

'Perhaps she senses that I'm harmless.'

Kathleen gave him an odd look and half turned to fiddle with a cleaning cloth, wiping it up and down the spotless draining board.

There was something about her gold dress that gave her skin an inviting warmth. It was warming him, too, the way it clung to her incredible body. There wasn't much left to the imagination—which was working overtime anyway.

He let out a long breath and sternly attended to the less destructive needs of his stomach.

'Good pie,' he said with far too much heartiness. He throttled back a few notches. 'Tender meat. Pastry melts in the mouth.'

With difficulty he banished thoughts of the soft liquefaction in his loins and focused hard on the act of eating.

'I think I'm hungry too. I didn't bother with supper,' she

said huskily, abandoning her aimless polishing. She collected a plate and sat down opposite him, then looked up from beneath her lashes and caught him watching her closely.

'Dieting?' His gaze roamed her figure hungrily before he could check it. 'I do hope not.'

She blushed. 'It wasn't that. I was a bit worried about you being out all that time,' she confessed.

Her hand was shaking and he impulsively reached out to grasp it. 'Why?'

She looked startled. 'I—you... You rushed off so suddenly. And the last time you disappeared like that...well, you were very upset. I wondered what I'd done or said this time.'

'Nothing. I just needed to think. It's always been my way of dealing with tough situations. That's why I went off after hearing my mother telling Father she wanted a divorce. I had to think things through.'

'I understand.' She paused, then said, 'I feel terribly guilty because it was my mother who caused you grief.'

'Not your fault. I wish Father hadn't come after me, though.' Lorcan frowned. 'He knew that I could look after myself.'

'But he did search for you,' she said sorrowfully.

'Only because he felt he was totally to blame for everything that had happened.'

'Oh, Lorcan!'

He hesitated. Her sympathy and the look in her melting black eyes encouraged him to share those difficult moments leading to his father's death.

'He'd been forced to face the consequences of his adultery. What he'd once thought was exciting and illicit had become sleazy and shameful to him,' he said quietly. 'He saw what his blind infatuation had done to my mother and me and he was desperate to patch things up with her. And to tell me that he was full of remorse.'

She gazed at him with compassion in her eyes and he felt his heart muscle jerk.

'I never had a chance to say how sorry I was that you had to be the one to find him.'

'We made our peace with each other before he died,' he said gruffly. 'He told me…he was proud of me and that he loved me more than I'd ever know.'

'I'm so glad.' She was silent for a moment. 'I never believed you'd pushed him.'

'Virtually everyone else did. Harry was such a convincing gossip,' he muttered.

'You said…you'd gone off this time to think after seeing Declan and Bridget together,' she ventured gently.

It had been a bittersweet moment. A contented family, without a care in the world, absorbed in one another. Envy had torn at him, ripping open the hard shell that protected his emotions and laying them bare.

He wanted what Declan had. A woman and children who loved him. But he'd settle for the children.

He frowned, worried that he was becoming more emotionally involved with Kathleen than he'd intended. Out there on the beach his decision had seemed simple in concept and operation.

But she had a knack of drawing his feelings to the surface and muddying the plan. Relationships were tricky things. Concerned about his sense of detachment, he slipped his hand free and continued to eat.

'I needed to reconsider my plans,' he said in between mouthfuls. 'All these years I've been seriously wrong about you. I honestly believed that you were part of your mother's scheme to secure her future here. And I made a mistake about your relationship with Dec, too.'

He broke off. She was smiling, her face radiant. And he

was getting that indigestion again. Frowning, he rubbed at his chest.

'I know it's rather late coming,' he went on, 'but I apologise. I of all people should know that evidence can be misleading. I can't expect your forgiveness, the effects of my anger have been too far reaching, but—'

'Oh, Lorcan!' she said with a sigh. 'Of course I forgive you! You'd twice seen me in Dec's arms. I don't blame you for misunderstanding. But you see, he was the only one I could turn to when Mother and I were thrown out. He got me to Galway City and his aunt put me up for a while.'

It pained him that he hadn't been the one to help in her time of need but he kept his tone stiff and unemotional. 'It must have been traumatic for you.'

'Pretty vile. But I survived.'

'You were lucky to have Declan for support,' he said stiltedly. 'It sounds as if he's been a good friend.'

'Closer. Like a brother—' She broke off and winced, pursing her lips tightly, and his cool indifference vanished in a second.

'Kate?' he murmured in sympathetic concern.

'Oh, it's OK,' she said huskily. 'Just something my mother said. It's so shameful. I've never told anyone. You see, it's very likely that Dec *is* my brother—half-brother,' she corrected. 'Mother said it was more than possible. And Dec's father is convinced the dates tie up, though he's kept the secret for my sake.'

'My God!' Lorcan exclaimed in astonishment.

'Now you understand,' she said, her face earnest, 'that I could never in a million years contemplate a sexual relationship with Dec—or he with me.'

'You've had a hell of a time, haven't you?' he said, his mind whirling with the news.

'It's not been a bed of roses,' she said with a half-laugh. 'That's why I want to hang onto the happiness I have.'

'The Manor.'

'Yes.'

Lorcan let out a long, slow breath. He was almost there. It was more than he could have hoped for. The last vestiges of doubt were gone and the way was clear for him now. Smiling, he said, 'Talk about that later. Your pie's getting cold.'

Kathleen laughed with obvious relief and began to eat. She wiped a piece of flaky pastry from her lips just as he was contemplating removing it himself. With his fingers or his tongue. Lorcan clenched his jaw. Keeping control of his impulses was going to be difficult.

'Tell me about UNICEF,' she said, giving him a sly glance.

'Who told you that's who I work for?' he asked, in pretended surprise.

She went red. 'No one. I'm guilty of borrowing one of your videos. But I was making your bed up, you see and—'

'It doesn't matter. It's not a secret,' he said, amused by her embarrassment. Could she really be so transparently upright and honest, he wondered? 'I work as a lawyer on behalf of children,' he explained, pushing back his chair so that he could satisfy the cat's demands for affection. 'My team hammers out deals on behalf of the United Nations, usually where there's child labour involved, or problems with the harassment of beggar children.'

'That's why you were in Africa?'

'Yup. When I heard about Harry, I had to fly to Boston, get a team to take over my work, brief colleagues on my cases and nip over to Dublin. My feet didn't touch the ground,' he said wryly. 'I think half my body's still somewhere over the Atlantic. I could hardly stand upright when I finally arrived here.'

'I've been wrong about you too, haven't I?' she said softly. 'About you being a drunk, being a hard-nosed lawyer screwing clients for all you could get, and hating children—'

'Where did you get that idea?' he asked in astonishment.

'Con.' She looked solemn. 'You virtually ignored him until tonight.'

He squirmed a little. 'I didn't want to get involved. I thought you were using him to melt my stony heart,' he said with a wry smile. He pushed his plate away and leaned his arms on the table, mesmerised by the glorious warmth of her eyes. 'I love children. I've dedicated my life to them.'

Her breath drew in with a delicate little shudder. 'I could see that,' she said contentedly. Then she smiled. 'Seeing you on the video dressed as a clown at that party put you in an entirely different light!'

'Oh, that. We go in and win hearts and minds before making any investigation,' he said in dismissal. 'Did you get to the part where we filmed the children's working conditions?'

'No. I heard you moving about in here and turned it off. I only saw the party and those shots of you with those babies.'

Her voice had become low and throbbing with emotion. She seemed to sway towards him. Lorcan knew that he only had to stretch a little across the table and he could be kissing that lush mouth.

'It's a training video. I'd like you to finish it to see what I do.'

'I will. You were wonderful with those children, Lorcan,' she said softly, her eyes starry with admiration.

'I love my work,' he said gruffly. 'I'm pleasing myself.'

'Maybe. But you're doing invaluable work, nevertheless. I think you're a star.'

Breathing rapidly, he fixed her with his gaze, shaken more than he would have liked by the intensity of her words. He was finding it hard to focus his mind, which seemed to be fizzing elatedly because she had praised him unreservedly. Why that should matter so much, he didn't know. This was to be more of a business proposal than anything.

'I'm not a sadistic monster, then?'

'You couldn't be.' A slow smile warmed her face and eyes. 'Not the way you treated those kiddies. I think I was right and that you're quite a softie on the quiet.'

'I wouldn't go that far,' he said drily. 'But, as I pointed out before, you and I have always fought for the underdog, haven't we?'

Her eyes twinkled. 'And cats and rabbits and birds and—'

'Kathleen,' he said in amusement, interrupting what could be an endless list. 'We've learnt a lot about one another over the past few hours—all of it good. The situation is different now. I don't despise you—'

'And I understand you a little better.'

He smiled. For a moment he held his breath. And then took the plunge.

'Enough to share the Manor with me?' he asked softly.

It was exactly what she'd wanted, but she stared in consternation, not knowing what to say. Her heart had leapt with delight and she'd been on the brink of saying yes, but she was scared of rushing into a situation based on her instincts. They'd let her down too often in the past.

'In what way…*share*?' she asked cautiously.

'This house is large enough for both of us providing we're not at each other's throats,' he said with a smile that totally disarmed her.

Her eyebrow hooked up. 'Me in the servants' quarters, you in the rest?'

'I was thinking of something more…comfortable for both of us,' he said softly.

Her pulses pounded. Dry-mouthed, she said, 'For instance?'

'I think you know what I mean.'

'Lorcan—'

'Don't decide now,' he said quickly, overriding her husky croak. 'Why don't we see how things go for a few days and decide later? I do want to stay,' he said soberly. 'We're well suited, I think.' He grinned. 'You like cooking; I like eating!'

'Just like a man!' she teased. Half-disappointed, half-relieved to be on safer ground, she giggled and collected the chocolate *tartuffe*. 'We could give it a try,' she conceded.

'The pudding?' he asked hopefully.

'Sharing the Manor for a trial period,' she said with a scathing glance.

'But…could we share the pudding now?'

He was teasing her too! She laughed and divided it in two. 'Half for you, half for me.'

'It'll be good, I know it will,' he said softly.

'It had better be. There's a whole slab of prime quality chocolate in that!' she retorted, her eyes dancing.

'Beats yams any day.' He saw her questioning glance and explained. 'We always stayed in the villages whenever we went to Africa, and brought in a lot of food to help out, but we seemed to end up eating yams, nevertheless.'

'Tell me about it,' she begged.

'I don't think—'

'Please,' she said quietly.

Reluctantly he agreed and she listened with fascination while he talked. They finished their puddings and then moved to the drawing room with a glass of brandy each. He became more expansive as he described the day-to-day problems and she wondered if this was the first time he'd ever gone into detail about his work.

Her eyes rarely left his face. He spoke with passion and sincerity, as if his job was his sole reason for existence.

Gradually she realised this was true. She built up a picture of a man who'd abandoned any kind of personal life at all. Every waking hour had been spent working for the cause of oppressed children.

Because he was on an unstoppable flow of speech he didn't pull any punches and several times she was in tears. Lorcan would then silently pass her his handkerchief and wait for her to recover while he stroked in turn the three cats who were now making themselves at home on his lap.

'I'm sorry,' she said, sniffing after one harrowing description. 'I don't know how you can cope with some of the things you witness.'

'I've had practice in containing my emotions,' he said, looking at her over the rim of his glass. He finished his brandy. 'And I'm not much use to the children if I break down in tears. They're living the life; I'm not. I have to stay calm and in control because if I keep my head, I can make a difference, Kathleen. That's what spurs me on.'

He was amazing, she thought hazily, her eyes captured by his.

'I'm going to leak information about you,' she said quietly. 'The village will get to know what you're really like. They'll think you're the fairy on the Christmas tree by the time I'm done.'

'I sincerely hope not!' he protested, but she could see he was pleased.

She swallowed. He was looking so happy. Fighting a desire to push the cats off and take their place so she could hug him, she said, 'It's better, surely, than being the local villain. You've been treated unfairly and someone has to put people straight. I can't bear injustice.'

'Come here, Kate,' he breathed, stretching out his hand. And then the lights went out.

She discovered that she'd been holding her breath and let it escape in a rush. 'Nothing to worry about,' she said shakily, feeling for the table to park her brandy balloon.

'I wasn't worried,' came his warm, rich growl. 'I happen to like the dark.'

By the flickering fire she could see his eyes. Was it her imagination, or had he moved nearer to her? Prickles of awareness ran up and down her spine and suddenly she felt nervous.

'We can't sit here like this!' she declared with painfully false cheeriness.

'Why not?'

Because, she thought, it was too compromising and too intimate. 'I might need to go to Con,' she retorted. 'I'll light the candles.'

'All right. If you like, I'll check the fuse box for you.'

There was an odd thickness to his voice and she stiffened. How many brandies had he consumed? As she became acclimatised to the dim light, she saw he was pushing the reluctant cats off his lap and half rising.

Nervously, she leapt to her feet and put the table between them, keeping a wary eye on him while she lit the candles on the mantelpiece.

'Be careful. The wiring's tricky,' she said edgily, pushing one towards him and maintaining a safe distance.

'My hands are steady,' he said quietly, holding them out to show her.

She felt awful. Harry's drinking had made her paranoid. 'I'm sorry,' she mumbled, avoiding his gaze.

'Being wary of a man's mood has been a part of your life for a long time, hasn't it?'

'It's hard to adjust,' she admitted, touched by his understanding.

His sudden grin slashed the darkness of his face. 'Come and watch me do my electrician act. Decide for yourself if I can drink a glass of brandy without destroying my fine reflexes and bursting into a chorus of ''Nellie Dean''.'

'Idiot!' she said, laughing.

He held out his hand. If she refused it he'd be offended—and she'd already virtually accused him of being too drunk to see straight. So she picked up the candelabra and slipped her hand into his, enjoying the little sharp stab in her chest as the electricity sparked between them.

That was funny, she thought. She could probably light a whole room with the energy firing between them!

They went into the hall and she found the fuses in the drawer of the ornate hat stand. Lorcan climbed up on a chair, checking the fuses one by one in a calm, methodical manner. Kathleen watched, refraining from pointing out that she'd become a whiz at fixing them over the years.

'Ah. This one. Lo, there was light!' He jumped down, beaming with success, but she was wishing for the romantic pale moonlight again. 'Reflexes all in perfect working order.' He gave a wicked smile. 'Peter Piper picked a—'

'Yes! All right, you're sober!' she said wryly. 'Don't make me feel worse than I already do! And…thanks. I'm relieved it was nothing more than a fuse. I was afraid the wiring had given up the ghost. Well, I'd better be off now. Goodnight.'

'So soon?'

She fidgeted awkwardly, wishing the evening could go on for ever.

'I think so.'

'Then goodnight.'

For a brief few seconds, his hands were on her shoulders and his warm mouth was touching her cheek. A small quiver betrayed her.

There was a brief pause when the tension in the air rocketed to saturation point and then his lips had slid to hers, her hands were cradling his head and her senses were leaping to a state of full alert.

Part of her wanted the inevitable to happen. She clung to him, kissing him desperately. He looked fevered and determined. If she wanted, he would make love to her. And she wanted.

Breathing heavily, she eased away. Too many alarm signals were sounding.

'Goodnight, Lorcan,' she whispered shakily.

He rocked on his heels but released her, his eyes glittering.

'Sleep well. See you in the morning,' he said politely, and headed up the stairs.

CHAPTER EIGHT

SHE was heaving seaweed into the link box on the tractor when she next saw him. Wearing jeans and an open-neck shirt in an eye-boggling orange, he walked across the pure white sand towards her. She felt her heart flutter and her hands become clumsy, as if they were carrying far too many fingers.

Picking up the pitchfork she'd dropped, he said cheerfully, 'Can I help?'

'Please! Be my guest!'

Kathleen sat on a lichen-encrusted rock, quite delighted by his relaxed manner. Lorcan took one look at the seaweed, another at her sandy, weedy wet sweater and without warning stripped off his shirt and placed it on the tractor's bucket seat.

There wasn't a spare ounce of flesh on him. Only hard, toned muscle, the skin tanned and satiny. Quite without shame, she ogled him as he started lifting and stacking seaweed as if there were no tomorrow.

'What exactly am I doing this *for*?' he shouted, without breaking rhythm.

'It's cheaper than going to the gym and it amuses me!' she retorted with a grin.

He turned briefly, a load of glistening brown weed on the fork, and advanced, a mischievous look in his eyes. 'Is that so?'

'Don't!' she yelled, and ran off squealing as he thundered after her. But she was cornered against the rocks. 'No!' she protested, giggling. 'Please! I'll smell dreadful!'

'Penalty, then.'

Heat raced through her. Without taking his eyes from her, he placed the fork on the sand. Her heart began to thud with anticipation.

'What?' she forced out.

He took his time replying. 'Spend the day with me.'

She looked down to hide her disappointment that he hadn't wanted to kiss her breathless.

'If I must,' she said, off-hand. 'But I'm working.'

'No problem. We need to spend time together if we're to judge whether we can share the Manor,' he said reasonably.

'True.'

Skilfully he forked up the heap of weed again and they began to walk across the glistening wet sand, disturbing a flock of ringed plovers. She and Lorcan stopped and watched the birds whirling and swooping in unison over the water's edge, their liquid notes echoing across the bay. The plovers settled again on the strand, running a short way and then stopping, their heads bobbing up as they kept an eye open for danger.

'Who wants stress management,' Lorcan said contentedly, 'when there's all this?'

'Stress management?' she queried. 'Down here we go fishing.'

He chuckled. 'We must do that together.'

'I'm too busy.'

He frowned. 'Surely you have some time off?'

She raised a dark eyebrow. 'A single mother with a job and an estate to keep going?'

'Then I'll work with you so you do get some leisure time.'

'Leisure?' She wrinkled her nose playfully. 'Never heard of it.'

He put his free arm around her shoulder. 'Well, you have

now. What are your plans for today?' he asked, when they'd reached the tractor.

Enjoying the feel of his friendly embrace, she gave a deep sigh of pleasure.

'First, I'm taking this back for the garden. You can ride on the ledge of the link box if you like.'

'Then what?'

'I'm taking some sample veg and pies to a new hotel on the Sky Road. Then I'm having a picnic and buying a few things in Clifden, then I pick up Conor and put the washing on, then he comes along with me in the evening while I do a yoga class in the village hall and then I do the ironing.'

He rolled his eyes. 'Exhausting schedule. Forget the yoga. Come out to dinner with me instead.'

She smiled. 'Forget it? I'm teaching it!'

'Dinner tomorrow, then. Get a babysitter,' he coaxed, retrieving his shirt and tying it around his waist.

It had been years since she'd been out and she couldn't help the grin of pure delight. 'Lovely,' she said with glee. 'Thank you!'

Happily she leapt on the tractor and started it up before Lorcan's melting gaze completely robbed her of the ability to breathe. And she pushed back the little warning voice. It was no big deal. They were going to have a pleasant afternoon, and tomorrow evening she was going to be wined and dined. That was all.

But her spirits were irrepressible, her optimism high and she began to sing with joy. Lorcan joined in. Amused by his complete lack of pitch, Kathleen turned to laughingly complain. The words died on her lips. His eyes were closed and his face was transfixed by happiness as he bellowed into the crystal-clear air.

Hastily she turned back again and drove the tractor up to the road, bewildered by her reaction. Wanting to stop the tractor and fling her arms around him in tearful rapture, squeezing him till he gasped for mercy, she began to sing again, her voice soaring pure and true into the still morning air as they chugged slowly along towards the Manor's entrance.

'This important contact you're making at the hotel,' he said idly when they'd stacked a mountainous pile of seaweed by the compost heaps. 'Will that be with or without bladderwrack?'

She followed his pointing finger and looked down at herself in dismay. Laughing, he started pulling bits of it from her hair. Her startled vision was suddenly filled by his torso, all golden and flecked with scraps of weed. She stepped back quickly before her fingers began to explore its contours.

'You're no better,' she protested. 'Race you to the shower!'

With Lorcan and the dogs kicking up a shocking din behind her, she darted into the house and up the back stairs, but he beat her to the bathroom by a few seconds.

'Whatever happened to ladies first?' she asked reprovingly, when he stood grinning triumphantly in the doorway.

'Died out when political correctness came in,' he said, and shut her out.

Pretending to grumble, she went to her room and fetched a change of clothes. She returned just in time to see Lorcan emerging from the bathroom, with a towel seemingly the size of a facecloth just managing to meet about his lean hips.

She wanted to stare but knew what decent girls did, so she pursed her lips and ostentatiously averted her eyes. Lorcan did like to live dangerously!

'I left the bath towel for you,' he said in amusement.

'I brought my own,' she said haughtily, and dashed into the bathroom, wondering if his rich chuckle was infectious. She certainly couldn't stop grinning!

But then, she mused, as the shower washed off her morning's work, it had been far too long since she'd had fun with an adult, especially of the fooling around kind.

'I'm coming out. Are you decent?' she yelled through the door when she'd dressed.

'Sadly, yes. Superficially so, anyway,' he called back over the barking of the dogs.

'Right.'

She marched out, determined to behave as normally as possible, despite the fact that he was a hunk—now in an eye-catching turquoise shirt—and there was a bed within tempting distance.

'Wow! A dress again!' he said admiringly.

'It's for the chef. All chefs like legs,' she said in defence of her choice—a blue V-necked dress cinched in tightly at the waist above its flirty skirt.

'I must learn to cook,' he mused.

She giggled. 'Um…if you don't mind, I have to dry my hair here. It's the socket—I get a better view in the mirror—'

He came forward, his hand closing on the dryer she was waving about. 'I'll do it. Sit down.'

'But—!'

'Sittt!'

Meek as lambs, she and the dogs promptly sat, and he laughed, driving her more surely towards total adoration.

Having her hair dried by him was one of the sexiest things she'd ever known. His fingers lifted her hair, touching the nape of her neck and sending delicious thrills through her entire frame.

Soon she stopped worrying that he'd make a hash of it and closed her eyes in bliss. He knew what he was doing all right. He'd done this for other women. Her teeth snagged at her lip as jealousy ripped through her body.

'Scowling doesn't suit you,' he drawled.

She opened her eyes and saw her own sulky face in the mirror and Lorcan's wickedly dancing eyes.

'I'm wondering what you'll charge,' she lied tartly.

He grinned. 'For a mop of hair like this? Top rates.'

'Duck with wild berry sauce?' she suggested.

'Done!'

'My! You're easily satisfied.'

His fingers stilled. They exchanged glances. 'I wouldn't say that,' he said softly.

Overcome by a hot, burning hunger for the feel of his mouth on hers, Kathleen lowered her lashes. 'Hurry up,' she croaked.

'We can't go on like this,' he said in her ear, threading his hand through the still wet ends of her hair. Wide-eyed, she stared at his reflection. He smiled lopsidedly. 'We must get the plumbing and electrics overhauled. We can't keep using the same bathroom.'

'The cost—'

'I'll sort it. Leave it to me. Now. Let's see…'

To her alarm, he had turned the dryer off and was bending over her, tucking her hair behind her ears. His fingertips grazed the soft skin there and every nerve in her body became instantly electrified.

'It's fine,' she said, jumping up. 'Thanks. You're very good.'

'I used to do my mother's, when she had a frozen shoulder for almost a year,' he said huskily.

Kathleen blinked, remembering Mrs FitzGerald's pain and frustration, a slow smile spreading over her face. 'You were very good to her,' she said. 'But Lorcan…we've got to dash.'

'No tip?'

'Chamomile's awfully good for a nervous stomach,' she advised solemnly.

Lorcan chuckled. 'Come on. Let's go and land you that order.'

That day, they both behaved like eager children. High up on the fabulous Sky Road, with its stunning views across deserted bays and islands and with the backdrop of mountains, they drove and sang and chattered, stopping to leap out and exclaim over the scenery, the Mediterranean-blue sea, and lush green land.

Kathleen's exuberance must have communicated itself to the hotel chef she visited, because he enthused satisfyingly over her vegetables and baked goods and put in a regular order, which had her gasping with delight.

Because she was shaking like a leaf, Lorcan drove them to the picnic spot she'd chosen. It was her favourite—a small, deserted Caribbean-white beach with a fifth-century ruined monastery at one end and a megalithic tomb on the sheltering hill behind.

She virtually danced along the path to the strand. 'I can't believe they've given me such a lucrative contract—and that they think their sister hotels will be interested!' she said excitedly as he tested for wind direction with a wetted finger.

'Here.' He put down the picnic basket and spread out the car rug. 'It won't be too much work?' he asked, investigating the contents of the hamper. 'You don't have enough time to yourself as it is—'

'I'm hoping to expand,' she said confidently. 'I think I can now bump up production big-time and offer piecework to an ex-cook in the village. The baker's near retirement and more than happy to rent out space. Kevin will take over most of the baking and leave me free to work outside. He's even better than I am at pastry.'

'Impossible,' said Lorcan, his mouth full of Kevin's Stilton and prune pie.

'I'm *so* happy!' she cried fervently.

'Me too.'

'Are you, Lorcan?' She met his warm, lingering gaze and stopped breathing.

'What sane person wouldn't be,' he said, breaking the hazardous mood that had developed, 'in a part of the world as beautiful as this?'

To his relief, she stopped making his heart race with her ecstatic smiles and turned her attention to the food, her eyes lowered and out of harm's way. For a while she seemed subdued and he was glad because it took the pressure off him.

So he leaned back contentedly, watching a lone heron peering hopefully into the shallows.

'I'm off for a walk,' she said abruptly. 'Alone.'

She was a pleasure to watch, at one with the landscape. There was a certain sadness about her as she strolled along the shoreline, her small figure less upright and vigorous than usual. Vulnerability was a big part of her appeal. She needed taking care of.

He sat up, scowling, a hard lump forming in his chest as his conscience briefly flashed questions at him. Like...shouldn't he encourage her to find a man she loved, and would his plans for her deny her a chance to be truly happy?

His brain raced as he packed up the picnic. As though a string attached him inexorably to her, he stopped and turned to observe her as she came back towards him. The wind was blowing her hair away from her downcast face and he was tempted to do something stupid to make her laugh because...well, no one liked a sulky face, did they?

Hell. Who was he kidding? He wanted to make her happy. And he could. They both wanted to live at the Manor. There was only one way to achieve that without being branded sinners by the whole darn village.

And, he thought wryly, if she agreed to his suggestion,

he'd know for sure that she'd made a level-headed decision based purely on security and material needs.

Love wouldn't enter the equation for either of them.

They took the bog road back, through the vast peatlands, between glassy mountains polished by ice ages and past the hundreds of dark, mysterious loughs coloured chocolate-brown by the peat.

Kathleen didn't speak but that didn't worry him. It gave him a chance to mentally move back from her. And so he absorbed the wild beauty of the scenery with greed.

Clouds lay like shawls on the mountains. Rivers cascaded down the sheer slopes and bubbled over boulders beside the road. Ruins dotted the landscape: early Christian churches and, more sinister, the remains of whole villages which had been wiped out in the great famines of the last century.

This land was part of his soul, he thought, profoundly moved. And he was unable to help himself from slipping a glance at Kathleen as she drove and thinking that this was another wild beauty he would be happy to look at for the rest of his life.

Any man would prefer beauty, wouldn't he? Her profile fascinated him with its pert little nose and generous mouth. There was a rosy glow on her cheek from the sun and wind and a small dusting of sand as if she'd rubbed her face. His glance flicked to her fingers, which held traces of glittering mica and silica, and he found himself smiling in affection.

No. Liking, he amended with a quick frown. He liked her. She worked hard and didn't shirk tough, mucky jobs. That he admired, as he'd admire it in anyone. Anything else was sentimental tosh.

While Kathleen was taking her yoga class that evening, he kept an eye on the duck, as he'd promised. Though what he was looking *at*, he didn't know.

In between puzzled peeks at the oven, he set the scene for his seduction. Working fast, he polished the fruitwood table in the dining room, laying it with the best silver and glass. From the cellars he chose the perfect wine and placed it on the Georgian silver coaster then dashed out to pick enough roses to fill a crystal bowl.

'Lighting,' he mused, critically checking the effect of the chandelier. 'Not intimate enough.'

Several candelabra were lit, casting a subtle and magical glow. And then he prepared the drawing room, lighting the fire, setting candles in the sconces and choosing mood music to waft over the speakers through the house. The room had never looked lovelier. How could she resist?

His mouth felt dry. His fingers trembled. And as he showered and shaved rapidly he realised just how important this was to him.

Aftershave. Not too much. Which shirt? He stared blankly at the Technicolor assortment, quite incapable of deciding.

Black or red would be sexy but a tad too obvious. Unused to dithering, he played safe and picked the solitary white linen one, teaming it with a lightweight navy suit and frowning with irritation when his fingers made a hash of fastening the belt.

Back in the kitchen, he found himself listening for Kathleen's return and irritably sang along with the romantic ballads drifting over the sound system. But his ears were cocked, nevertheless. So he sang louder.

Seeing the cheque in the fruit bowl, he hesitated, then picked it up and tore it into tiny pieces.

'Hi, there! We're back!' she called, suddenly appearing in the doorway.

He had to slick his tongue over his nerve-glued lips. 'That's quick,' he lied.

He kept staring, dumbstruck. She looked as radiant as a

bride. Who'd caused that? Flames of jealousy flashed to his brain before he could stop them.

'Wow! You're…' She blinked, her eyes huge, her red lips parted over dazzling teeth. There was a long pause. 'Very smart!' she finished brightly.

'It's an occasion. We're celebrating your success with all the pomp and circumstance we can provide,' he explained, suddenly worrying that he'd gone over the top. 'Looks as if you had a good time,' he observed, fishing.

'Wonderful! Energising and relaxing at the same time. You must try it,' she said blissfully, taking the sleeping Con into the housekeeper's room. After a moment she came back, peeling off her warm jacket and setting the baby alarm.

With commendable self-control he managed to stop gaping at her figure-hugging leotard top, but the damage to his body was done in the first fatal seconds. If doing yoga meant he could look at her in that outfit for an hour…

'I'll enrol immediately,' he said, aching with instant desire.

She beamed as if he'd presented her with a valuable gift. 'How's the duck?'

'Dead. A kind of orangey brown,' he said helpfully.

With a giggle, she opened the oven door and poked the bird. 'You've done well. It looks fine.'

'Piece of cake,' he told her airily, extraordinarily pleased with her praise. 'Now I can do yams *and* duck *and* bread and butter.'

'Idiot!' she said with a laugh. 'I think the duck can come out now,' she said, slipping her hands into a pair of oven gloves. 'It needs to rest.'

'Why? Is it tired?' he enquired innocently.

Kathleen threw back her head and laughed, her eyes bright and sparkling like diamonds in black velvet. It was

all he could do not to catch her roughly there and then and
to hell with the meal and the romantic setting.

'Terminally,' she replied with a giggle. 'Meat is more
tender when the fibres are left to cool and relax for a while,'
she explained.

'Oh.'

He couldn't get enough oxygen. The breath was short
and high in his chest and he had to snatch air through his
mouth.

She seemed to be fascinated by his parted lips. He
wanted to check in the mirror to see if he'd left shaving
cream on them, but she'd abruptly turned away and so he
stole a few moments to admire the long line of her neck
with its kissable tendrils of black curls and the infinitely
touchable curves of her back.

'I'll get the veg on,' she said in an odd scramble of
words, 'then I'll take a quick shower if you think you can
cope with steaming pans.'

They'd go with his steaming body, he thought wryly.
'Many people at yoga?' he enquired, determined to find the
reason for her elation.

'The usual.' In a graceful, feminine gesture she unconsciously patted the glorious mass of hair which she'd piled
on her head and clipped with a large yellow object rather
like a designer bulldog clip. 'Twelve of us. Oh, plus Dec's
cousin from Roundstone who brought a couple of mates.'

Men! They'd take one look at Kate's body in that leotard
and be like raging animals!

'Decent sort of guys?' he hazarded, hoping they were
sub-human and totally unlikeable, with not a scrap of libido
in the whole of their bodies.

'Female sort of guys,' she said with a smile.

He despaired at his relief. But then realised it was natural. He didn't want anyone muscling in on his plan. He

intended to win himself a family without all the pain of risking a courtship and a rejection.

'We're eating in the dining room,' he said casually. 'I've set the table.'

Her face lit up. 'Lorcan! That's a great idea!' she cried, her face lighting up. She ran to see what he'd done and he followed. 'It looks gorgeous and I feel very pampered,' she said, turning to him in admiration. 'Thank you for making the effort. My favourite music, too. Now make sure the veg don't boil dry. I must do a quick transformation scene and change from the Ugly Duckling into—'

'Cinderella,' he provided. 'Don't be long. Your prince awaits.'

If only, she thought as she scuttled into the house-keeper's room. It would need a fairy godmother with an enormous wand to turn her into a beauty.

She knew, however, just the dress for the occasion. It was her Christmas party outfit: second-hand but a gorgeous rich red, with a deep scoop neck and no sleeves. The long, narrow skirt hugged her body beautifully and had a rather daring slit, but she could conceal that by moving carefully.

Getting ready was a scramble, and she only had time to twist her hair up again and fasten it with star-shaped dia-manté clips and to refresh her lipstick. In the kitchen next door, she could hear Lorcan singing in his terrible, off-key voice, and she smiled happily to herself, adoring it, as she dabbed a little perfume on her pulse points.

'Fabulous,' he said in a gratifyingly husky voice when she emerged, alarmingly out of breath. 'You're knocking me as dead as the duck!'

'Thank you. I think.' Strangely awkward, she picked up the carving knife.

'Wait a minute. Can't ruin that dress.'

Lorcan brought over an apron, slipping it over her head.

The soft warmth of his breath whispered over her bare neck and shoulders as he clumsily fastened the ties at the waist.

She knew that she only had to turn around and they would be kissing. The air pressure between them thickened and swirled around her, making her movements slow and languorous.

'You'd better carve,' she whispered, afraid she'd cut her fingers off. 'I'll do the rest.'

And she slid an apron over *his* head, deliberately letting her trembling fingers slide down the smoothness of his tightly clenched jaw. Confronted by his broad expanse of muscled back, she gulped and quickly fudged some kind of knot at his firm waist before moving away, dazed and astonished by the devastating effect of being near him.

This had never happened before. Ordinary tasks had never been difficult in the presence of other men.

Shaken by her response, she avoided even the smallest glance in his direction, her face solemn as she concentrated on the once simple job of dishing up a meal.

'Ready,' she said in relief, covering the final serving dish. And before he could offer, she hauled off her own apron. She looked at the food and realised she didn't feel like eating. Her appetite had completely vanished.

'I'll carry the heavier tray,' Lorcan said quietly.

At the dining table, busying herself with serving the meal, she relaxed a little. Lorcan began to talk about his plans for the house, explaining that he wanted to set up his European office in the east wing and provide accommodation in the village for key workers, perhaps even developing some of the unused outbuildings on the estate.

Kathleen could immediately see the benefit to the community and she felt more convinced than ever that their partnership would be successful.

'Please start,' she coaxed, when he seemed reluctant to eat too.

Lorcan took a mouthful of meat, then closed his eyes briefly in bliss. 'Oh, paradise!' he groaned. 'I thought I wasn't hungry,' he marvelled. 'But this is superb. You must teach me.'

'Yoga? Horticulture? Cooking?' she said with a shaky smile, hoping he wouldn't notice her plate remained untouched.

'All of them. And I'll teach you in return.'

She stopped pushing her food around, her hand suddenly weak. 'What? Law?' she asked in a ridiculous squeak.

'Well...everything I know,' he murmured wickedly.

Unable to quite believe the message in his eyes, she countered with a quick defence. 'Oh. A short study course, then!'

His eyes twinkled and he raised his glass to her. 'We've always had the same sense of humour, haven't we, Kate?' he said happily.

'I suppose we have! I've never thought of it before.'

Suddenly she felt hungry after all and began to eat. 'Tell me more about your plans for the future,' she said eagerly.

'I've thought it all out. The great thing is that we're *totally* compatible.' He reached for his wine and sipped it, watching her intently.

Her heart turned over. 'We are?' she croaked.

'Perfectly. Your venture is ideal to continue alongside mine and complement it. For instance, we'd all need feeding at lunchtime—and what better than produce from the garden—plus Kevin's baked goods?'

The heavy beat of her pulses subsided and she put aside her disappointment as he expanded his ideas. Yet his scheme excited her and his enthusiasm was enchanting.

The candlelight flickered on the planes of his face and she stared at him longingly, a feeling of dizziness overtaking her as he listed the jobs there would be for local people.

'...and we'll need local craftsmen to work on the alterations.' He leaned forwards earnestly. 'You can trust me not to do anything to spoil the integrity of the house. But I think there's a lot of potential in the old stable block and the orangery. One more thing. There would be the occasional function—parties for visiting dignitaries and lawyers, the odd dinner. I'd like you to be my hostess, Kathleen. What do you say?'

His dazzling smile made her heart lurch alarmingly. 'I'm not used to entertaining grand people,' she hedged, faintly unnerved by the idea.

'It's no big deal. One, you are beautiful. Two, you care about people and are interested in them. Three, you've always made any party come alive just by being there. Four, we'd be on our home ground. Five, we'd do this together, as a team,' he finished softly. He waited for her to say something but she was too stunned to speak. 'I can't think of anyone I'd rather ask,' he said huskily.

'I...' It was no good. She couldn't formulate her feelings of delight and amazement that he thought so highly of her.

'A yes will do.'

Still dumb, she nodded her head and was rewarded with his melting smile. 'Wonderful!' he breathed. 'So we go ahead with our plans?'

'Of course.' Finding a little croaky voice, she raised her glass in salute. 'To your European office.'

'And the expansion of your business.'

Her head reeling, she made no move to stop Lorcan clearing the plates and dishing up the bread and butter pudding. Almost everything she'd dreamed of was coming true, she mused, pouring the orange and whisky sauce on her portion.

In a happy daze, they discussed the order of priorities and she began to realise at last that the burden of maintaining the Manor was now to be shared. And she felt free for the first time in years.

'If you've finished,' Lorcan said casually, laying down his napkin, 'we could go into the drawing room. I've made up a fire in there. I'll do the dishes in the morning.'

He was by her side before she could move, one hand on the back of her chair. 'You're spoiling me,' she said with a contented sigh.

He tucked the baby alarm in his pocket. 'I think it's time someone did,' he replied, taking her hand in his.

This is wonderful, she thought, her eyes pricking with happy tears. All their antagonism had gone. He respected her and she…she loved him. Involuntarily her hand tightened in his grasp and he gave it a little answering squeeze. Their eyes met: hers molten and shiny with wonder, his tender and as deep as the ocean.

A questing finger angled her chin and he dropped a light kiss on her mouth. 'Thank you for enabling my dreams to come true,' he said in a low tone.

'Mine are well on their way too, because of you,' she whispered.

'Good.' He kissed her again, and she felt the tremor in his body that echoed hers.

'Lorcan—' she began in a strangled voice.

'Come on,' he said quietly, leading her into the drawing room. 'Near the fire.'

Weakly, willingly, she was being borne towards the vast sofa. 'Lovely,' she said inanely, tucking up into one corner.

The firelight gave a glistening sheen to his tense jaw, and her eyes devoured him from the top of his golden head to his elegantly shod feet. With long and lingering pauses in between.

He was gorgeous and sexy, crusading for underprivileged children and kind to dumb animals. A man to admire. To love.

Her dark eyes followed every move as he plugged in the baby alarm. She felt as nervous as a kitten, sensing his intention to make a pass. Despite her fears, a delicious excitement invaded her head, making it buzz as if she were intoxicated.

'Dance with me,' he said softly, coming to stand directly in front of her.

'D-dance?' she repeated, stalling for time till her mind cleared. Held close to him. Feeling every inch of his body. 'I don't think so.'

'Please. You're not afraid of me, are you?' he murmured.

'No, but...' She saw that he looked dismayed. 'It's just that—'

'Please.'

How could she refuse? Uncertainly, she looked up from beneath heavy lids and found herself holding out her hand in mute compliance.

Immediately she was drawn to her feet and pressed firmly, irrevocably to his body. With a sigh of pleasure, he closed his eyes, curving his palm against the back of her head so that her face lay against his upper chest where his heart pounded with a touchingly unsteady rhythm.

Imperceptibly they both moved to the slow, sensual music, each step tightening Kathleen's body as Lorcan's hips swayed with hers and the hard shaft of heat swelling against her pelvis became impossible to ignore.

She had a choice and she knew it, as all women do. To move away, or to stay.

Just as she was about to push Lorcan away with some excuse about Con, Lorcan's mouth pressed softly into her temple and her intention was hijacked.

The hand which drove her body into his had begun to slide with agonising slowness from the small of her back towards her tightly clenched rear. She could smell the cleanness of him and the tantalisingly subtle fragrance on his skin.

This was the moment to break free, to play safe and keep

her heart intact. He wouldn't need more than a hint. He was a proud man and sensitive to rejection.

Her eyes closed of their own accord because Lorcan was kissing her neck with such a gentle savagery that it made her moan aloud. Too late, she thought, as passion flashed into every pulsing vein. Too late!

Her arms wound around his neck and she stared drowsily into his sultry eyes as they swayed together. Lorcan trailed a finger across her forehead and then kissed the line of each eyebrow. There was a small bead of sweat in the hollow of his throat and without thinking she enclosed it with her mouth.

The heat of his skin and its satin texture was like an aphrodisiac to her lapping tongue. As if in a dream, she unbuttoned his shirt and pulled it aside so that her open mouth could settle on the angle of his collarbone. Slowly her lips explored the bone, her fingers lightly spreading over the hard wall of his chest.

No one had done that to him before. And it was a kind of divine agony. He could barely breathe for desire, all his senses focused on the moist softness of her inner lips as they dragged seductively over his skin.

Half-crazed with need, he buried his face in her slender neck, tasting her, not daring to move his hips a millimetre in case he completely lost all self-control and ruined the delicious pain of prolonged anticipation.

'Kathleen,' he murmured hoarsely into her small ear.

Her head tipped back, luring his mouth to swoop on the silk of her throat. This was more than he'd ever imagined in his wildest dreams, he thought muzzily, nibbling at the slender line of her jaw. Sex was to have been earthy and satisfying. This was something else. He could lose his mind in Kathleen's arms.

A brief hint of danger sounded in his head.

But he was too hungry to call a halt. Slowly, with infinite

care, he kissed her, opening her mouth to his and feeling the blood throbbing more urgently in his loins as his tongue slid into the sweet moistness of her.

With a groan, he drew her to the thickly carpeted floor and drove his mouth down on hers possessively, sliding a finger beneath the strap on her gleaming shoulder to hook it off. She tensed, but his kisses swept away her protests. And as she writhed luxuriously, his other hand encountered flesh on her thigh: firm and smooth and firing his heart madly so that it hammered with violent beats in the depths of his chest.

A multiplicity of sensations dazzled his brain. Her demanding mouth and panting breath, the swell of her breasts gradually being exposed to his marauding fingertips, the sound of her skirt as he slowly pushed it out of his way.

She was making little moaning noises, her eyes half-closed in ecstasy, the lines of her face so lovely that it hurt him physically, bringing a lump to his throat.

'You are so incredibly beautiful,' he breathed shakily.

'Oh, Lorcan!' she shuddered, her voice just a little zephyr of a breeze against his lips.

Beyond control, Kathleen let her eyes flutter shut as his palm closed on the naked mound of her breast and one of his fingers began very lightly to sweep back and forth across its fiercely swollen centre. Needles of desire radiated out to the rest of her body as the peak became more and more engorged and formed into a tiny knot of aching tension.

'Please!' she mumbled incoherently. 'Please!'

Incapable of bearing it any longer, she caught his head in desperate hands and forced him to take a straining nipple in his mouth.

A long, low groan jerked from her trembling body as he suckled her, tugging and releasing the hot, hard peak and letting it slip moistly from his mouth before capturing it again.

The gentle tenderness as he did so and the sight of his rapt face reached deep into her emotions. Without any shame or awkwardness, she slid down her other strap and wriggled her dress to the waist, longing to be naked, to feel his body on hers…in hers.

'Oh, God!' he whispered helplessly. 'I never knew you were so perfect.'

Her heart lurched. With smouldering eyes, she lifted her hands and pushed up her high, firm breasts to him. Willingly he touched her, kissed each one, nuzzled the soft, hot slick of skin beneath and licked each trembling tip with the flickering tip of his tongue.

And all the time her body was aching, waiting for his wicked fingers to reach the top of her thigh. In a fit of aggression, she ripped at the buttons of his shirt, stretching up eagerly to take each of his flat, hard nipples in her mouth. Lorcan flinched and groaned, pushing her hand away, his eyes blazing with hunger.

'Don't,' he said hoarsely. 'I need you too much, want you too much. I'm crazy about you, Kathleen!'

She felt a wash of love flood through her. Shaken by her feelings, she closed her eyes.

I love you, she repeated to herself, lazily arching her body. His mouth descended on hers and she realised when her hands touched his back and his body pressed against her that he'd stripped off his shirt.

'I'm crazy about you, too,' she murmured passionately, adoring the feel of their bodies, flesh to flesh. She shimmied from side to side, revelling in their nakedness.

With a muttered exclamation, he spread her arms above her head and kissed from each fingertip to each breast in turn, ignoring her protests, ignoring her attempts to entice him further by making her taut nipples rub against his.

And then in one movement he slid her dress away and his lips were everywhere on her body: her waist, her hard, flat stomach, hips... And now, tormentingly, his teeth were grazing her pelvis as she jerked and moaned beneath him, demanding with every move of her body that he should make love to her, *now*.

It was surely the beginning of their relationship, a life of loving, she thought. Every touch, every gesture suggested that this wasn't a casual seduction but that he felt as deeply as she did.

She sighed extravagantly as she felt the flick of his thumb expertly identifying the small, fierce concentration of pulsing sensation between her legs.

They would be lovers, and then he would realise he loved her. She had no doubt of that, even though her mind was on another plane. She felt it in her very being and because of that she felt free to surrender to her clamouring passions.

'Yes!' she breathed, clutching at his shoulders and digging her fingers into his back. 'There... Go on, don't stop...'

Her head thrashed from side to side as her silky dampness allowed his finger to dive between the petals and slip across the sensitive nub in a delicate and relentless rhythm. She was out of her mind. Floating, crying, moaning, begging.

There was a pause and then, after an agonising moment when she thought he'd abandoned her, his warmth had returned and she felt the tip of his hot shaft pulsing against her thighs.

Her eyes opened slumbrously and she touched him, caressing the throbbing smoothness beneath the sheath barrier and encircling it with her hand, gently putting pressure on as she slid her hand up and down.

'No!' he groaned thickly. 'Too good. Please, Kate...I want to make love to you fully.'

She answered with a kiss and guided him into her, all the breath expelling from her lungs as he slipped smoothly in and her whole being echoed with the thought *At last, at last!*

From that moment she operated on a purely physical level, unaware of what she did, knowing nothing of her uninhibited passionate responses or her husky, urgent cries, until she reached somewhere quite different.

The depths of her emotions bloomed and dazzled her with the overpowering realisation that this was the man she had always loved, and would love to the end of her life.

For the first time ever, she was climbing to the heights of physical and emotional and mental experience, every part of her body pulsing feverishly as Lorcan murmured incomprehensibly in her ear and pushed her beyond all endurance.

At last she reached the pinnacle of ecstasy and found herself shuddering as the climaxes thundered through her small frame, on and on as her body tightened around him in quick, urging spasms which made him cry out and shake his head, the sweat slippery and lubricating between their arching naked bodies.

In a series of slow releases, they both finally juddered to a halt and then subsided, their bodies replete, every muscle and sinew at a point of exhausted peace.

So this is how it feels, she thought, stunned by the perfection of Lorcan's lovemaking. Then came the 'little death' she'd heard of, the moment of blankness, a brief emptiness. And afterwards the love came flooding back and she felt her heart leap with joy when he put his arms around her and drew her close.

They didn't need to speak. His feelings were demonstrated by the way he almost crushed her to him and how

he kept murmuring her name, over and over again in an
infinitely tender voice, thick with emotion.

Her hand stroked his face, soothing him because she
could tell from the trembling of his body that this had been
special for him too. Perhaps, she thought drowsily, just before she fell asleep, he'd been shaken by emotion too.

When he carried her to the shower and gently soaped
her, she hardly woke, hanging onto his neck like a limp
doll. Talking to her like a sleepy child, he dried her tenderly
and tucked her up in bed, then tiptoed away. She smiled
blissfully and promptly fell asleep.

CHAPTER NINE

IT RAINED the next morning. Amazed to see that the dishes had been done by the time she rose at six, Kathleen struggled out to see to the animals and hurried back, hoping Lorcan would be in the warm, dry kitchen, looking smug and making jokes about lie-abeds.

Happily she chatted to Con, who was playing on the floor, but Lorcan didn't show his face till after ten, by which time she'd given up waiting for him and was well and truly deep in her monthly wrestle with columns of figures.

When he came in, she looked up, smiling warmly. 'Thanks for doing the dishes. Disturbed night? Or did you sleep like a log?' she asked innocently, her eyes sparkling with wicked lights.

He gave a tight little smile and went to collect the kettle, saying perfunctorily, 'Disturbed.'

It wasn't the answer she was expecting—or the response she'd imagined. A cold hand clutched at her heart.

'It's my indoors day,' she said warily, watching him keenly as he organised his breakfast. 'Doing the books.'

Lorcan acknowledged her remarks with a grunt. 'I'll probably be spending the whole day on the phone,' he muttered.

Her dark eyes blazed at his detachment. 'Are you having regrets about last night?' she asked bluntly.

The cup in his hand rattled and he put it down quickly, at last meeting her gaze. 'No. Oh, no,' he replied, his voice oddly harsh.

'Then why the cold shoulder?'

'I didn't know how *you'd* feel.'

She smiled with sympathy. He really did fear rejection. 'Me? Ecstatic,' she declared, risking everything.

Then at last a slow answering smile unravelled the taut muscles of his face and he came over to Kathleen, bent and kissed her mouth.

'Me too.'

There was a brief caress of her head and then he had removed himself to the end of the table. Kathleen frowned, puzzled by his reluctance to be near her. Perhaps, she worried, he'd only wanted sex after all and was uncomfortable with being affectionate in the cold light of day. She reined back her bubbling happiness and sobered up as a precaution.

For a few moments he was engrossed in admiring Con's proffered Jack-in-the-box and then he said, 'I'll take my breakfast in the library, I think. I'm late starting and there's a lot to do.'

Disappointed, she nodded, outwardly cool and casual. 'Lunch at twelve-thirty suit you?'

'Don't bother doing anything for me.' He was already piling toast and cereal onto a tray. 'I'll come and do a sandwich when I'm ready. Pretend I don't exist,' he added, pushing the door open with his shoulder. And with an almost curt nod of his head, he was gone.

At first she was shattered, immediately jumping to the conclusion that he'd used her. He'd needed sex and she'd been there. For a few moments her mind was in turmoil as she relived their lovemaking in minute detail.

And her taut muscles began to relax when everything pointed to the contrary. Maybe he hadn't given any verbal indication of his feelings—other than lust—but surely he'd been too caring and too considerate to have been intent only on satisfying his own needs. In her heart of hearts she believed there was something deeper between them.

Lorcan had spent years denying his emotions. It would be a while before he opened up. If she showed him how much she trusted him, and shared her feelings with him, then maybe he'd do the same.

'You,' she said to Con, kissing him around his sweetly scented neck and blowing a raspberry or two, 'will never have difficulty expressing your feelings. Love Mummy?' she asked tenderly.

'Mmmmm!' said Con, obliging with a huge wet kiss on her nose.

'Yes, well,' she said with a grin, 'we'll have to work on your technique a bit before you start dating girls!'

Dashing in distractedly to make a cheese sandwich—and being easily persuaded to add a slab of cold local salmon and fresh raspberries to his sparse tray—Lorcan reminded her of their dinner date at a Galway restaurant.

'Dress up,' he advised.

'Posh, is it?' she asked, excited.

'Finger bowls with the beefburgers,' he replied deadpan.

Delighted that his sense of humour had surfaced, she opened her eyes wide in pretended astonishment.

'*That* posh!' she marvelled, and his face cracked in a small smile before he turned and left the room. She wondered what was bugging him and hoped he'd been shaken by the emotions of the previous night—then immediately checked herself for being over-optimistic and fanciful.

Bridget came in later to babysit, greeting Lorcan cheerfully and rolling her eyes at Kate's emerald-green top and hip-hugging skirt.

'You look different,' she said, narrowing her eyes critically.

Kathleen flushed, knowing Lorcan had shot her a quick warning look. 'It's the lipstick. Almost as bright as Lorcan's shirt, isn't it?' she said perkily, diverting attention to his coral eye-blinder which he'd teamed with a honey-coloured suit.

'I think we should go before you both persuade me to wear nothing but taupe and donkey-brown,' he said drily and, with a smoothness that was admirable, he'd swept Kathleen out before Bridget could make any other telling remarks.

'Do I look that different?' Kathleen probed, when they were in the car.

'Less harassed, perhaps.'

She bit back the urge to ask if she wasn't more beautiful, womanlier than before and made herself be content. She'd fallen in love with Lorcan as he was, warts and all; if he never trusted her with his heart then she could hardly complain. He was what he was.

The restaurant hummed with activity, chatter, sophisticated people and attentive waiters. Lorcan managed to command the personal service of the maître d', who placed them at a discreetly private table and obviously recognised a man with authority and money when he saw it. Even if, Kathleen thought with a giggle, Lorcan's date was somewhat below par!

'This is fantastic,' she declared, as their first course was removed. 'I feel like a real person again, Lorcan, instead of a mother, cook, gardener and bottle-washer.'

'I want life to be easier for you,' he said, taking her hand.

Delighted with his unprompted gesture, she let her fingers close around his. 'I don't mind hard work—'

'I know, but—'

He paused, waiting for the maître d' to pour their wine. Then their main courses arrived with surprising swiftness and Lorcan seemed to forget what he'd been going to say and applied himself to his haunch of venison.

Gently, biding her time, she turned the conversation to his plans for the house and they discussed colour schemes and furnishings eagerly, arranging to shop in Galway the next week.

'I want you to take on help with the vegetable garden,' he said, expertly cracking a lobster claw for her. 'I'm engaging a full-time gardener for the estate. I think we should talk about staff for the house—'

'Wait a minute!' she said, alarmed. 'Who's paying? We must clarify who does what and where—'

'That's what I wanted to talk to you about. When the pudding comes. We won't be disturbed then.'

Mystified, Kathleen waited and tried to imagine what he had on his mind. Something that made him uncomfortable, she decided. Her nerves began to make her jittery. Lorcan hadn't referred to their lovemaking once. He hadn't said anything particularly complimentary or lover-like. He'd been courteous and strangely detached all evening, except when expounding on the future of the Manor.

She drew in a steadying breath when her caramelised lemon tart arrived, and pushed it to one side, leaning forwards to buttonhole him and nail her doubts once and for all.

'What's the matter?' she asked flatly. 'You've been peculiar all day.'

Lorcan fixed her with his piercing sea-green eyes. 'Nothing.'

'There is,' she insisted. 'If we can't be honest and upfront with one another, if we can't feel comfortable together—'

'I have a proposition for you,' he said abruptly.

Her hand went to her locket as her stomach clenched. A proposition. Just what Harry had said. With a premonition filling her with dread, she looked at Lorcan enquiringly, unable to speak.

'We get on well. We…' There was a quick dart of the tip of his tongue as he wetted his lips. 'Last night…'

'Yes?' she encouraged, desperate for some kind of feed-back.

His eyes smouldered, setting her alight. He rested his hand on hers, stroking it hypnotically, and she felt herself melting beneath his ardent gaze.

'I've never known anything like that, Kathleen,' he said throatily, choosing his words with care. 'I didn't know that a man and a woman could experience physical sensations so…profound and moving.' His voice thickened. 'Even talking about it arouses me. In fact, I've spent all day trying to crush the memories so I can get on with some work!'

Kathleen's eyes kindled and she smiled, relieved to know the reason for his strange behaviour. 'You should have said,' she murmured. 'I would have found a way to relieve your suffering.'

'I want you,' he said simply. 'Every minute of every day. That's part of what I want to say.'

Her mind reeled. 'Lorcan!' was all she could manage.

'The other… The other thing I have to say is…'

He kissed the tips of her fingers and a spasm of love arced through her body. *Say it,* she urged silently. Say the words. Tell me you care. I know you do. We've always been made for one another. Say that. Tell me…

She forced herself to stop hoping too much.

'Yes, Lorcan?' she whispered.

His chest rose and fell several times as if he was steeling himself to some dreaded task. Kathleen smiled with affection. Surely it wasn't that hard to admit your feelings!

'I would like you to marry me,' he said in a rush, snapping his eyes up to meet hers.

She stared back at him in blank amazement. He was serious. There was no twinkle of amusement in those fathomless eyes.

'Say something,' he growled.

'I—I didn't expect… I didn't think you…'

Something stopped her from continuing. Lorcan had dropped his gaze as if he felt awkward. It boded ill. Surely he should be declaring his love, or if that was beyond him he should at least be pleading silently with her and maintaining contact. As it was, he'd dragged his hand away and was sitting back in his chair, regarding her with a steady and penetrating stare.

'What do you think?' he asked quietly.

She shivered, suddenly chilled. 'Why?' she asked, her lips horribly dry. And she waited for his answer, fearing that it wouldn't be what she wanted.

Lorcan inhaled deeply before meeting her wary eyes again. 'We both want to live in the Manor, yes?'

Kathleen gave an imperceptible nod. Now what? she wondered, beginning to tremble, hoping against hope that he wouldn't come up with the arrangement she was imagining.

'That doesn't mean we have to marry,' she croaked at last.

'I disagree. People will talk if we share the house—'

'I don't care!' she breathed.

'But what about Con?'

Her brow furrowed. There would be talk. In this remote and upright community people would be shocked. Con would suffer as soon as he was old enough to know what other children and adults were saying.

'We could divide the house in half without any access from one part to the other,' she suggested.

Lorcan's gaze scorched her skin. 'You think we could keep away from one another after last night?' he said quietly.

'We'd have to.'

'Do you want that?' He leaned across the table, crowding her, his hot gaze creating havoc in her body. 'Don't you want to repeat what we did? To be touched, kissed, aroused—'

'Stop it!' she whispered, horrified by her fevered reaction to his murmuring voice.

'You want me.'

She hesitated too long, her eyes too dark with desire, and he gave her a small smile which said that he knew how much she desired him. But his suggestion was abhorrent. Pained, she knew she had to say so.

'Lorcan, I—'

'Listen to me,' he said persuasively. 'If we are married then you automatically have security of tenure. I'd take on all the expenses of the house, which we can renovate as our marital home. You'd be wealthy, Kathleen. You and Con need never worry about money ever again. Ballykisteen will be your home and your child's. His future will be assured and so will yours.'

'A commercial venture,' she said in a dull voice, thinking, With sex thrown in for both of them. Did he think she was mad?

'Not exactly. There's more. Something else we both want.'

Her head felt as if it was weighed down by lead and she raised it with difficulty. 'Go on.'

Infuriatingly he fiddled with the cutlery for a while. Eventually he said in voice laced with huskiness, 'I've always longed to have children of my own. I can't think of anyone I'd rather have as their mother other than you.'

He couldn't have hurt her more. She had frozen in her chair, her eyes huge and hurt, something sharp and searing ripping at her heart and guts. No mention of love. A marriage of convenience because of the gossip and because he enjoyed the sex and wanted children.

Most ironic of all, it was an echo of Harry's arrangement—but with sex thrown in. All stated in cold, clinical terms. An offer of material wealth and an emotional desert.

The chatter in the restaurant had become a loud buzzing which filled her head with whirling sound. An iron band seemed to have clamped around her chest, squeezing out the air.

She had misjudged Lorcan as she'd misjudged all the men with whom she'd formed personal relationships. He'd pursued her because he'd wanted sex. And then, she thought bitterly, after he'd tested her out and decided he wanted more, he'd seen how well she'd fit into his need for a baby-machine for the wretched FitzGerald dynasty.

Her body felt as if it was turning into solid ice. Once again she was being asked to consider a loveless partnership. And all that entailed.

'Kathleen?'

Slowly she lifted her eyes to his and felt as if her heart would break. She loved him so much and yet he didn't care at all for her feelings.

'No.'

He went pale. 'I'm making a hash of this,' he said tightly. 'Bad timing. Bad setting. I should have asked you somewhere else, where I could take you in my arms—'

'I want to go,' she breathed, afraid she'd break down in public.

'Of course.'

The maître d' came at his nod and in a few moments Lorcan was helping the shaking Kathleen to her feet. He draped her coat around her shoulders and attentively ushered her to the car, his arms firmly around her because her legs seemed like jelly.

She remembered nothing of that drive back, only the huge hole in her body and the darkness outside.

'I'm all right!' she snapped irritably, pushing him away when he came to assist her to the front door. She pressed a hand to her pounding forehead. 'Deal with Bridget. Tell her I've got a headache,' she ordered, and went to curl up out of her friend's sight in the drawing room.

When the sound of footsteps told her that Lorcan was escorting Bridget home, she stumbled to her room, where Conor lay asleep.

Sinking to her knees by the cot, she put her hand through the bars and stroked his thick dark hair. There wouldn't be another marriage without love. Her son mustn't grow up in such an atmosphere.

When she told Lorcan that marriage was out of the question, he'd be offended and he'd ask her to go. Her heart was heavy. They were back to square one.

Her back stiffened at the soft knock on the half-open door. She heard Lorcan come in but he said nothing.

Wearily she rose and aimed her dulled eyes at his midriff. 'We'd better talk, I suppose.'

He opened the door for her to pass. Although Con would never hear them, she didn't want to conduct this difficult conversation in the kitchen, so close to her innocent son, so she headed for the drawing room where she took up a position in front of the softly glowing fire, leaning for support on the mantelpiece.

Lorcan's expression was unreadable, but his jaw was tight and his eyes cold. Kathleen summoned up all her courage, quashing the little voice which said that she loved him, why not have what he could offer?

'Your suggestion is unacceptable. I can't consider a marriage without love,' she said bluntly.

He flinched, visibly, his mouth pressing into a hard line. 'You did with Harry!'

Kathleen rocked on her feet. 'Yes, and to my great regret—other than the fact that Conor was the result,' she answered. 'I can't do it again. It was too painful.'

'I thought you cared,' he said in a flat tone. 'I had the impression that you did.'

She didn't dare answer that. 'I don't like being a business proposition,' she cried, driven beyond all caution. 'You think that I should be grateful, I suppose! The housekeeper's daughter, offered the position of wife! How dare you treat me like this?'

'A wife is a better position than a mistress!' he shot like a whip.

'Not if it means living out a lie!' she retorted, her eyes flashing hotly.

'A lie? You said you were crazy about me—'

'You said the same about me!' she blazed in despair.

'I know, and I say it again!' He stood there, his body tense with passion. 'I want you. I need you!'

'Tough!'

'You're not immune,' he growled. 'Your whole body is on fire—'

'How do you know?' she challenged.

'I can feel it. My skin is tingling with the static in the air that we're generating. Your heart is beating hard, your face is flushed, your eyes are sparkling—'

'In anger!' she cried desperately.

'In desire,' he insisted. 'What if I removed my tie…?'

'Don't!' she whispered, her pulses jerking erratically as he slowly eased it free, his eyes never leaving hers.

'Why? It shouldn't bother you. You feel nothing for me, remember? I could even slip off my jacket…undo the buttons of my shirt…'

She had to swallow hard before she could speak, and it was a tell-tale gesture which made his eyes glow with hunger. 'Don't…do this!' she mumbled, frantically crushing her terrible longing to surrender, the memories of his touch and the wonderful sensations filling her body unmercifully.

'Do you expect me to base a relationship on mere sex and financial convenience?' she croaked.

'It's a start,' he said quietly. 'We get along well—'

'*Oh!*' It was the final straw. She turned her back on him before he saw her tears. She ached for his love, to be gathered in his arms and to hear him say he would love her till he died. Even a lie would perhaps have swayed her; she knew that she wanted to be with him so badly that she might have believed him, however insincere he might have sounded.

'I won't marry you,' she grated.

'Then we will live together in sin.'

'No!'

'You know the alternative. You'd be tearing Con away from his birthright.'

She pounded the mantelpiece with her fist. 'Why do I have to be the one who leaves? I want *you* to go! You managed without living in Ballykisteen all these years! Why can't you walk away and be done with us?'

She felt the warmth of his chest against her back, resisted the urge to lean into him and looked up with a tragic expression, meeting his eyes in the mirror as his arms wrapped around her.

'Because of last night,' he said simply.

'Sex,' she muttered despondently.

There was a small pause. 'The most powerful reason in the world.'

No, she thought, love was more powerful still. And yet she couldn't deny that the feel of his body, and the small but wickedly arousing kisses feathering her neck, were acting as a powerful aphrodisiac and slowly weakening her resolve to stay aloof.

Why shouldn't she please her basic desires? She ate, didn't she? Laughed, craved friendship, good company, the love of her child... Why should she deny herself another pleasure—providing she remembered not to give Lorcan anything else other than her body? She'd make sure that he'd never sire her child or know that she loved him. But for a little while she could ease her painful primitive needs.

Lorcan had turned her in the circle of his arms and was kissing her so passionately that she hardly knew what she was doing. With every desperate, heart-aching plunder of her mouth she felt her resistance melting.

'Please don't!' she mumbled unhappily.

And he released her at once, his face suddenly shuttered.

Without another word, she stumbled blindly to her room, unable to think for the awful nothingness shrouding her whole being. There was no answer to their predicament that would satisfy them both and make them content. None at all.

Almost a week later, they were still in a kind of limbo, nowhere nearer to breaking the deadlock. Both of them had used their workloads as an excuse not to alter their strange, side-by-side living arrangement.

A team of decorators were working on the exterior of the house. Men were scrambling over the roof, repointing the chimneys and securing loose gutters, and she was providing a steady stream of tea for them—and for the electricians and plumbers working inside. It was bedlam, and welcome, but Kathleen knew that the activity meant Lorcan's plans were going ahead. He had no intention of vacating the Manor and soon she would have to pack her bags and go.

In the village, there was much gossip about the goings-on at the big house, but not in the way they'd both feared. Kathleen's situation saved her. Everyone knew that Lorcan had come to claim the Manor and she would be evicted. At first, her determination to stay had been admired, though

Lorcan's plans were beginning to create some divided loyalties.

One or two people asked why she didn't move out and she began to dread that inevitable moment, since she'd have to leave Ballykisteen itself, because she could never live in the same village and see him every day. That meant leaving Bridget and Dec too, jeopardising her business...

Kathleen groaned. The ramifications were huge. How could she deal with them? Every day she went over and over the situation, trying to find a solution till her head ached with her teeming thoughts.

Her gloom increased. Lorcan put on the pressure, coaxing her, painting a rosy picture of their lives together.

'Marry me,' he said every night.

'Don't ask!' she begged, but was sorely tempted. This wouldn't be like marriage to Harry. She loved Lorcan, and sometimes when he looked at her she imagined that he felt as affectionate towards her as he could ever be to any woman.

Everything in his past had taught him to protect his feelings. Maybe he couldn't give any more of himself because his capacity to love was too deeply buried.

Maybe, she thought despondently, she was kidding herself and he'd opted for a woman who was good in bed, cooked like a dream and was fertile enough to produce a child on demand. How could she ever know the truth?

Over dinner, at the end of the tense, fraught week, she studied him carefully. For a little while they'd forgotten their troubles and had shared the joy of bathing Con and putting him to bed.

Several times during the week she'd almost thrown caution to the wind and accepted Lorcan's proposal—just because of the marvellous way he treated her son. Watching them together was a delightful agony. This was the man she would have chosen above all others to be her husband, to father her children.

This was the man she ought to reject if she had any common sense at all.

Moodily she sipped a glass of mineral water, wondering for the millionth time if she could risk marriage to Lorcan. He'd make a fantastic father—Con adored him and his little face lit up when Lorcan was around.

Kathleen stared at her untouched plate. Her fear was that Lorcan would eventually meet someone he did love. And then what would happen to Con and her—and any child of the marriage?

'You're very quiet tonight,' he said, breaking in on her turbulent thoughts.

She wouldn't look at him. 'There's a lot to think about.'

'I know,' he said gently. 'And I've been thinking too. I have an idea. Why don't we move Conor to the bedroom next to the master suite? You can choose the paper and paint you like and I'll pull a couple of men in to decorate the room, put up shelves and a toy cupboard and so on. He deserves a proper nursery.'

It sounded wonderful. But she might be gone by the middle of the week. 'He's all right where he is,' she said stubbornly.

'I disagree. Wouldn't he be better in a room with animal friezes and cartoon characters on the walls instead of beige wallpaper? Somewhere for his train set and girlie posters?' he murmured.

'Girlie posters?' she scoffed. That suggested a long stay! It was impossible, couldn't he see that? Anger tightened her mouth and she wouldn't be amused. 'That's not why you want him there,' she muttered. 'If Con is next to the master suite then I'd need to be close by.' She glared at him. 'Closer to you.'

'Well, it is cramped in your quarters,' he reasoned. 'You

deserve better as Harry's wife, and Con certainly should live well as his son. I'm keen to give him the best nursery in Ireland. Murals on the wall. Mobiles. Clowns abseiling down the chimney-breast. Whatever you like.'

Seeing her closed expression, he left his chair and squatted on his haunches beside her, his hand on her thigh. She shut her eyes momentarily as her pulses rocketed.

'I would also like you nearer to me,' he confessed. 'I want you in bed with me, all night. I want you in my arms, sleeping. To wake with you beside me. To reach out and feel you there—'

'To give you a child.' Misery had made her snap that out in a hard, scornful tone. 'You'd be just a stud. I'd be—'

'That's enough!' Lorcan stood up, his eyes glittering as he gazed down at her. 'You're not in a reasonable frame of mind. I think I'll have an early night,' he added in a strangled voice.

'No! Wait!' She jumped up, twisting and folding her hands in a ferment of indecision. But she couldn't bear to see him so hurt, and she'd been foul. 'I'm sorry,' she mumbled, her eyes filling with tears. 'I'm confused and tired. This is an awful situation. It has to be resolved. I must go, I know that, and the sooner the better—'

'Move in upstairs with me,' he said softly. 'It was your bedroom once, after all—'

'No, never. It—' Her hand flew to her mouth but it was too late.

Lorcan had stilled, his whole attention riveted by her thoughtless disclosure. 'Are you saying that you never slept there?' he asked, ominously quiet.

She bit her lip and dragged it through her teeth. 'That's right.'

He snatched in a ragged breath. 'But you and Harry...'

'I slept down here,' she said, hoping he wouldn't pursue that any further. 'It was safer. With him drunk so often.'

A dark cloud shadowed Lorcan's eyes. 'Of course,' he said shortly. His head lowered as if in defeat. 'I'll go up, then. Goodnight.'

'Not yet. I don't like you to be angry with me. Lorcan,' she pleaded, 'I want us to stay on good terms. Please help me here. You must see that I can't go on like this any longer. I—I must get out of here, and I want us to part as friends because I c-couldn't bear it if...' She couldn't speak for tears.

He stopped in the doorway, his back to her, its expansion telling her that he was hardly breathing. 'You're saying things I don't want to hear. I don't want you to leave and yet I can't stay close to you without wanting to touch you,' he said through his teeth. 'And since you're not interested in a long term relationship I think I'd better start to get used to the idea.'

'But I do want that,' she whispered to herself.

And yet he heard. His head came up and he slowly turned to face her. 'What was that you said?'

'Nothing—'

He strode towards her. 'That's not true. Tell me what you said!'

She shrugged, not caring any more. Her dreams had long died. 'I want the relationship,' she said quietly.

He frowned, puzzled. 'Then why reject it?'

'Fear.'

'I'd never harm a hair of your head!' he said passionately.

'I know that. I'm afraid of the consequences. It would have been easy to agree if I only wanted material comforts and just enjoyed sex with you,' she said bluntly.

'So what's the problem?' he probed.

She gave a small, rueful smile. 'The problem is that I love you, Lorcan. And because I love you I want to be loved in return, not treated as a sex object and a convenient baby-producer!' Her unhappy eyes met his. 'Don't you see what you are doing to me?' she cried, close to weeping.

'You…love me?' A range of emotions was crossing his face and she wasn't sure if he was pleased, puzzled, disturbed or horrified. 'Kathleen!' he cried gutturally, and before she knew what was happening she was being crushed to his chest and the life was slowly being squashed out of her.

'M-m-m-m!' she protested tearfully, half suffocating.

He eased his hold with a laugh, cradled her face in his hands and gently kissed her. 'There is no problem any more. Marry me,' he said passionately. 'Tomorrow. The next day. Soon. But marry me! I'll make you so happy, Kathleen. You know I'm crazy about you. Marry me. Say yes.' He kissed her. 'Yes!' And kissed her again. 'Yes, yes, yes!' he whispered against her compliant mouth.

'I won't!' she mumbled.

'You, me and Con together. I'll take care of him, be a father to him. We've had some good moments as a family, haven't we?' he murmured.

She looked at him helplessly. 'Yes, but—'

'I promise you this,' Lorcan said softly. 'I will never let you down. I will never need any other woman—'

'That's easy to say now. What about in ten years' time, when I'm fat and I've got wrinkles and the children are being a pain and—'

'I am making a commitment to you and to our marriage,' he said soberly. 'If we should have difficulties in the future then we'll work through them. I have no intention of being unfaithful. I know the consequences of such behaviour only too well. I am very serious about this, Kathleen. I will never hurt you in any way. I swear this on my father's head.'

And the warmth of his mouth melted into hers in a kiss so tender and sweet that she moaned in hopeless defeat and whispered a weak and trembling, 'Yes!'

*   *   *

For the next two weeks, Kathleen spent her days choking back her doubts, her life one whirl of activity as their wedding was announced and arranged in the midst of all the alterations to the house.

Only occasionally did she pause for a moment and confront her fears. He hadn't once said that he loved her. Of his passion, she had no doubt; he proved that every night— and in sudden, spine-tingling moments during the day. It wasn't the same as love, though.

She wasn't sure if she was kidding herself or not, but Lorcan *behaved* like a man head over heels in love. He touched her constantly, kept glancing at her. His face softened with a gentle radiance whenever she appeared and he took a delight in giving her thoughtful little treats. Their lovemaking seemed to be much more than mere sex. But that could be wishful thinking on her part.

Perhaps stupidly, she hoped with all her aching heart that it was just a matter of inhibited emotions that prevented him from uttering those special, longed for words and time would ease his locked-up feelings.

And after calming her nerves with that comforting thought, she found herself worrying that she was just wishing for the moon and he would unwittingly break her heart.

CHAPTER TEN

KATHLEEN tensely watched a pied wagtail bobbing about in the rainswept garden as she tried on her wedding dress in the master bedroom. The wagtail reminded her of the little bird whose broken wing she'd tended. It had flown to freedom, soaring happily over Doo Lough and, hopefully, returning to its mate.

Alone in the sumptuous room, she slowly approached the cheval mirror, wondering if she was condemning herself to life imprisonment by loving a man who couldn't express his feelings.

Or who might not be capable of deep feeling at all.

She looked at herself. A bride-to-be, she thought with a fearful shiver at the enormity of what she was doing.

The dress had been chosen from a selection flown over from Boston. Her hands slithered down the simple, perfectly cut raw silk bodice. The smallness of her waist was emphasised by the swirl of the sumptuous skirt, which fell in elegant folds to a sweeping train at the back.

Trying to convince herself she was doing the right thing, she swivelled on the unfamiliar high heels, twisting to examine the daring swoop which bared her honeyed skin right down to the cluster of flowers at the small of her back.

Three days to go! she thought, her throat drying with nerves. The fourth of October...

With a cry of horror, she clutched at her stomach as it jerked like a jack-knife. It must be the first of the month today! That meant...

'No!' she moaned. 'No!'

Lorcan was simultaneously phoning the builder and

scratching Scruff's tummy when he heard her running down the stairs as if the hounds of hell were after her. Abandoning the dog, he rushed from the study in time to see her, dressed in her wedding dress and disappearing into the kitchen.

'*Kathleen!*'

His long strides swallowed up the ground. Fear made his heart knock at his chest. Above the sound of the rain beating against the window he could hear her crying in the housekeeper's room, a desperate, broken sound that he'd never heard before.

For a moment he hesitated, his body cold as ice. Then he cautiously pushed open the door.

She was on the floor, her skirts a pale cream sea of silk around her. She was rocking back and forth, and sobbing so hard that her body shook. To her breast she held a clutch of photographs.

'My darling! Whatever is the matter?' he murmured in alarm.

He knelt down in concern, her skirts a floating barrier which prevented him from holding her close.

Weeping, she turned away, protecting the photographs as if they were her children. He waited. And at last his patience was rewarded when she began to draw in huge, racking breaths and her body ceased to be ripped apart by her tears.

Ignoring her frantic protests, he reached over and drew her face around so that he could wipe her eyes.

'You must tell me what's upset you,' he said gently.

'I c-c-can't!' she sobbed.

'You have to. We can't have major secrets if we're to be married,' he said, trying to sound as reasonable as he could.

The pained expression on her face unnerved him. While he waited for her to speak, he tried not to think of the possible scenarios. But it seemed significant that she'd been trying on her wedding dress when she'd become upset.

He noticed that her hair had been piled on top of her head and laced with ribbons. She looked vulnerable and heart-rendingly lovely—and worryingly detached. A strange knifing sensation screamed through his body and for an extraordinary moment he thought his throat was tightening with emotion.

'You look unbelievably beautiful in your wedding finery, Kathleen,' he said huskily, subtly probing.

One hand broke its clasp on the photographs and tentatively touched the billowing silk. He relaxed. The wistful softness of her eyes suggested that she loved the dress—and all it meant to her.

'It's unlucky, seeing me in this,' she mumbled, and she shivered so violently that he slipped off his jacket and draped it around her.

'Superstitious nonsense. Now. Ready to tell me?'

She nodded dumbly and handed him the photographs as if they were fragile heirlooms.

'Conor?' he said, baffled, looking at them and handling them with great care.

'No.'

Alert now, he looked closer. Perhaps not. A child as dark as Con, with Kathleen's eyes, but... He watched her get up and sit hopelessly on the bed, sensing trouble, his quick mind coming up with something terrible. Another man in her life? Someone she'd loved enough to bear a child? Dear heaven! He couldn't cope with that...

Why? he thought. Why should that matter so much to him?

'Who?' he rasped.

She winced, fiddling with her fingers. 'Kieran.' There was an extended pause during which his throat tightened again with apprehension. 'My first son.'

His tensed muscles relaxed. A child she'd lost in her marriage to Harry. Sympathy coloured his voice.

'Harry's child,' he assumed, encouraging her to talk about it as gently as he could.

'No.'

Something held his stomach in a vice, his emotions see-sawing painfully as he fought the urge to shout the obvious question. He tried to conquer his breathing which was agony in his chest as jealousy tore through his body and drove away all rational thought.

'Whose?' he grated.

She shook her head as if she couldn't answer and the ribbons in her hair loosened a little, giving her a dishevelled appearance. Her arms wrapped around her body, pressing into her middle as if she too had an unbearable pain there.

Anger darkened his eyes and tightened his mouth. She should have told him! What other secrets was she hiding? Cold fear chilled his bones.

'I want an answer,' he said grimly. 'I think I have a right to know.'

She straightened. Her violet-shadowed eyes blinked at him and she knuckled away the tears in a determined attempt at normality.

'I met someone.'

'When?'

'When I left here and went to London,' she said dully, 'I was alone, with very little money.'

He was appalled, thinking of her starving, poor... 'So...what did you do?' he asked, his voice threaded with alarm.

'I didn't turn to prostitution, if that's what you were thinking!' she declared hotly.

He flushed. 'I was imagining you under railway arches with tramps, or begging in the street,' he said huskily.

'I managed to find a job washing dishes in a hotel.' She grimaced. 'It was awful.'

Forcing himself to ignore her forlorn tone, he persisted with his questioning. 'And you met someone?'

'A waiter. He...was very kind to me. He... I *thought* he was kind and loving—though it turned out he wasn't.'

'You fell in love,' he said, each word painful to utter.

'I thought so. I desperately wanted to be loved,' she admitted in a small voice.

Lorcan gritted his teeth. Typical. She'd needed love and fooled herself that she'd found it. Perhaps she was always chasing an illusion; perhaps, he thought in mounting horror, her avowed love for *him* wasn't real, either.

He said nothing, merely stared at her, and after a moment she roused herself again and began to speak.

'I found out quite quickly,' she said in a choked voice, 'that I was pregnant.'

'And he rejected you, I suppose,' Lorcan said scornfully.

'No,' she replied, to his surprise. 'He was delighted. He said we must marry as soon as possible.'

He felt the ice creep into his veins. 'And did you? Marry?'

'Oh, yes. I believed he loved me, remember,' she said miserably.

Lorcan drew in a sharp breath. So she'd been married *twice*! Two men had made love to her, taken her to bed, caressed her beautiful body and called it theirs, possessing it as often as they liked!

A million furious questions hovered on his lips, demanding to be answered. What was it like with this man? Did you cry out and shudder, did you have multiple orgasms with him, and did you burrow your head in his shoulder and sigh and whisper how much you loved him...? Lorcan blanked his mind to the torture he was putting himself through.

She'd ripped him apart with her revelation. Kathleen had borne two men a child, the ultimate gift of any woman.

It shouldn't have surprised him. He'd always known that she was quick with her affections. Too damn quick. What price her protestations of love for him now, he thought angrily, when love was something she felt for rabbits and injured birds and any impecunious waiter who happened to be kind to her?

She didn't know what love was. Her story had devalued what he'd believed to be special and now he couldn't trust her. Kathleen's version of love came cheap and easy. Not deep and heartfelt at all. Slowly his heart began to seal over.

'What happened?' he asked coldly. 'Why did he marry you if he didn't care?'

Her eyes flinched as if he'd hit her. 'Because he was a Libyan national. There was trouble over his papers and questions about our marriage—'

'He married you to get residence?' Lorcan asked sharply.

'Almost certainly.'

She hung her head, her hair falling from its ribbons and tumbling down to partially hide her tragic face, giving him brief glimpses of her downturned mouth and wet lashes.

'So?' he prompted abruptly.

A small shudder went through her and she burst into tears. He looked at her, willing himself to feel no compassion for her, knowing from his experience in practice what the probable outcome had been. The child had been spirited back to Libya and she'd never seen her husband again.

Wearily he turned to leave.

'You must hear what happened!' she wailed.

'I don't have to. It's obvious. When his application for residency failed he abducted your child and took him home.'

'Doesn't that touch your heart?' she croaked, sounding

astonished by his flat delivery. 'My baby was only nine months old! I was out of my mind with grief and worry!' she cried pitifully.

He clenched his jaw hard against the sympathy that welled up inside him. Images of women he'd defended in international abduction cases at the beginning of his practice flocked unbidden and unwanted to his mind. Their lives had been destroyed by the loss of their child or children and he'd had to steel himself not to become involved but to remain professional and lucid for their sakes.

It had been a terrible tragedy for Kathleen and all his instincts were driving him to console her. But he didn't dare. Her web would spin around him and he'd be caught fast. They'd marry in a whirl of compassion and passion and in a few years they'd regret every minute because her so-called love wasn't the kind that lasted.

'I've dealt with a lot of cases like yours,' he said with a shrug.

She gave a little shaky gasp. 'This is my baby we're talking about!'

His eyes bored ruthlessly into hers. 'Did you get a divorce?' he asked in a tight voice.

Tears were falling down her face, her eyes glistening brightly with them. 'I didn't have to,' she jerked. 'I had a message from the French consulate in Libya that my h-husband and my baby had died in a road accident. There was no contact address but these photographs were enclosed. I have one of him in my locket too,' she said hoarsely, touching the silver oval with a loving gesture. 'Today would have been Kieran's birthday. And for the first time ever, I forgot it!' she wailed, bursting into sobs again.

This was harder to cope with than he'd imagined and he couldn't keep the shock from his face. She'd been through hell. But he had to remember that her tragedy made no difference. They had to part—and the sooner the better. He looked at his shaking hands, baffled by the tumult within him.

She'd snatched away his dream. That was it. He'd seen himself as head of a family here. But…he could meet someone else, marry them, have a couple of children…

Lorcan dragged his lower lip through his teeth, astonished by his instant feeling of revulsion at that idea. Glowering at Kathleen, he wondered if it was because she possessed the same, raw sex appeal as her mother, and his male instincts were just protesting at the loss of the perfect bed partner.

A little voice nagged within him, saying that it was something more. And he scowled even harder, refusing to acknowledge any such thought. The implications were too far-reaching, too enormous to contemplate.

Kathleen saw his eyes take on a malevolent expression and with a cry of despair she scrambled to her feet, gathering up the masses of material of her skirts in her trembling hands. Before he could move, she rushed past him, frantic in her haste to reach the master bedroom and remove the wedding dress.

'Kate—!' he rasped suddenly, seeing her intention.

'Leave me!' she screamed, stumbling up the stairs. 'I hate you! You don't feel any compassion at all! You don't know what it was like!' she flung back. 'I was alone and ill and *empty*!'

He kept coming. Hysterical, she ran into the bedroom and tried to slam the door on him, but he shouldered his way in.

'Don't say anything!' she yelled, frantically twisting the little buttons at the back of the dress. She didn't want his contempt or his anger. 'I know I've been stupid; you don't have to spell it out to me!' she panted, furious that not one button had given way.

Her impassioned face lifted to his and she quailed. He looked so hurt, so horrified. She'd done that. Injured his pride, betrayed his trust. What a fool she was! He would never grow to love her now, never dare to admit any feelings he might have for her. It was over.

'Whatever I've done, I've always paid the price a thousand times over!' she cried hotly. 'You probably think I was "easy". That I'm my mother's daughter. Well, maybe that's true! I can't help falling for rotten men! I trust people, that's my trouble! Oh, damn this dress!' she said in utter frustration.

'Turn around,' he snapped irritably. 'I'll do it.'

'No! I don't want—'

'Turn around!'

Petrified by his unexpectedly barked order, she obeyed. Tensely she waited while he muttered with annoyance, foiled by six silk-covered buttons. And then she felt cool air on her lower back. She moved away with a briefly whispered thanks; the material whispered, and she stepped out of it and left it on the floor as if it meant nothing to her.

Not caring that she wore only lace briefs and bra, she tugged at the beautiful emerald and diamond engagement ring, which she'd chosen because the emeralds were the colour of Lorcan's eyes. Now her finger was bare—the wedding ring she'd worn as Harry's 'wife' already being in a box of Harry's which contained items she was keeping for when Conor had grown up.

'Here,' she croaked, jerkily stepping forward. Taking Lorcan's hand, she unpeeled his fingers and pressed the ring into his palm. 'I can't marry you. I won't marry you. And besides, I've deceived you more than you know.'

His whole body flinched, and his fist closed over the ring in a fierce grip which must have driven the precious stones into his hand, but he said nothing, only stared at her bleakly.

He hated her, she thought, her body full of pain. And felt a desperate urge to escape from those condemning, horror-struck eyes. With an abrupt movement, he pushed the ring into his pocket, turned on his heel and strode to the door.

'Where are you going?' she cried in agitation.

'Out!'

'It's a terrible night! You'll get wet to the bone—'

'What does that matter?' he said in an appallingly dead tone. And he chilled her with a glance, then stalked out, leaving her numb with shock.

Lorcan took the route he'd taken that other fatal day, when he'd found Kathleen in bed with Harry and his parents had decided to divorce. It seemed appropriate.

His intention had been to think the situation through rationally. Unfortunately his mind had other ideas. It appeared to be clogged up with unwelcome emotion and he couldn't focus for more than a second or two before he was thinking of the look on Kathleen's face, of life without her...

It was a revelation to him that sex had become so important to him. But their nights together had made an impact on his mind and body. He could see her now, smiling at him over the kitchen table, pouring tea for him...

Lorcan frowned. That was a domestic scene he was recalling, not moments of lust in bed. Almost immediately his restless mind flitted to the moment he'd seen her looking up at one of the builders on some scaffolding, her face rapt as he'd explained his technique for replastering the cornices. She'd been dressed in jeans and a warm, soft jumper, her hair a gleaming waterfall down her back. Con had sat astride her hip and she'd been jogging him rhythmically, the little boy's eyes drooping with sleep.

He stopped, oblivious of the rain which beat down on his unprotected head. Presumably he found that kind of woman sexy, he decided—that must be why he kept thinking of her in normal day-to-day situations. That would explain why he felt an overwhelming sense of loss whenever he pictured her and Con doing something humdrum.

She and Con... He saw them leaving Ballykisteen, suitcases packed into the back of a taxi, and had to grab at the low dry stone wall for support as a wave of hot nausea made him suck in his stomach. Groggily he dug his fingers into the moss and earth, trying to get his balance back.

Astonishingly, he could feel the sensation of tears clogging his sinuses and pricking threateningly at the backs of his eyes. With an impatient mutter, he launched himself into a power walk and for a brief time let physical activity drive her, and his demons, out of his body.

It grew dark. Knowing the paths so well, he was able to navigate his way home, and for a while he sat on the rock where he'd found his father, musing that they'd both made disastrous mistakes with the O'Hara women.

Kathleen wouldn't destroy him. His work would go on. But he would expand the international abduction division. Mothers—and fathers—and children must not suffer as she had. A way must be found to meet the best interests of the child in these cases and he'd devote his energies to doing so.

Normally this kind of decision would have elated him. But he was too depressed for his spirits to be lifted. Subdued, soaked to the skin and shivering with cold, he dragged his reluctant legs along the last few yards to the house and quietly opened the door.

It was the dead of night but a light was on in the hall. A sleeping figure was huddled on the bottom step of the sweeping staircase. Kathleen had been waiting for him, and he knew it was because she'd worried about him, out in the bad weather.

A brief and tender exasperation filled his heart before he

drove it away irritably. Did she never give up administering to the needy?

She appeared to be in her nightdress and cocooned in a blanket, though one hand was free and clutching a Thermos flask. Beside her was a sandwich on a plate and a piece of blackberry and apple pie. His mouth tightened as the affection came back more strongly, making a lump surge to his throat.

With a sigh of resignation, he crossed the hall and sat beside her, giving her a little shake. She murmured drowsily and opened her eyes.

'You're wet,' she said languidly, her fingers coming up to touch his dripping hair.

'Take your hand away!' he ordered through his teeth.

She was fully awake in an instant, her mouth quivering with hurt, her eyes enormous. 'No need to bark. I'm not a dog!'

'I'm sorry. I'm tired.' And on edge, he thought.

'I made some vegetable soup for you,' she said jerkily.

He frowned down at Kathleen, conjuring up visions of her standing in the kitchen, laboriously chopping up vegetables and cooking them with care. Guilt and confusion overpowered him and irritably he turned it to anger. He hadn't asked for this ludicrous self-sacrifice. What was she after, a medal?

'You *made* it? What's wrong with opening a tin?' he complained, knowing how unfair and ungrateful he sounded.

'I haven't got any. And I thought you'd be cold and hungry,' she explained, her expression reminding him of a wounded fawn.

'I am. That's why I'm going to take a hot shower,' he growled.

Annoyed with the lurching of his heart, he strode grimly up the stairs, his irritation increasing when she followed because he felt weak, and some mad urge inside him was tempting him to fall into her arms and let her care for him.

'What do you want?' he asked wearily.

'I'm making sure you have this soup,' she said sharply. 'But take that shower before you get pneumonia. If you're intending to make a habit of storming off during your life, choose a fine day or put some weatherproof clothes on and get in your darn car, but don't keep worrying people unnecessarily and causing them untold inconvenience!'

Kathleen banged the flask down on the table by the window and put the sandwich beside it. She wrapped herself in the duvet and sat down on the big chesterfield at the end of the bed.

Lorcan emerged from the bathroom granite-faced, wrapped in his own white robe. Expecting a battle, she relaxed a little when he sat down in the wicker chair by the window and began to drink the warming soup.

'Thank you,' he said curtly.

'No problem.'

Nervous, she pulled the duvet up to her nose and waited, knowing that during his walk he would have sorted out in his mind what he wanted to do.

'We must let people know the wedding's off,' he said at last, swivelling around to face her.

This had been inevitable, but it still came as a shock. Miserably she gave a quick nod of her head.

'I'll cancel the booking and alert the caterers in the morning,' she said glumly.

There was so much to do. All of it horrifying to contemplate. A small, sick feeling nestled unpleasantly in the pit of her stomach.

'You should have told me about your first marriage and your child,' he said, stiff and remote like a stranger.

'I know. But it…hurts too much. It's always there, in the back of my mind, and I try hard to keep it there because

I know I must move on, think of Con and the future, not the past,' she said forlornly. 'I've never got over losing Kieran and I never will. It was a terrible time,' she said with a shudder.

His eyes narrowed. 'Harry found you in London when you were grieving the loss of your child, didn't he?' he growled suddenly.

Nervously she met his blazingly intense stare, impressed that his legal brain had ferreted out the link that might lead him to extract the truth about Harry.

'He did. He was someone from a time when I'd been happy and I was overwhelmed to see him. He saw that I'd not been eating and was deeply depressed. I had no will-power. He talked of Ireland, the soft green hills, the un-polluted air and the pure white beaches, and I felt home-sick. He said he'd take care of me. I agreed to his proposition because I longed to be back in Ballykisteen with people I knew.'

Lorcan's mouth thinned. 'He took advantage of your low state of mind.'

'I suppose. I missed my baby so much! Even now...' Her arms instinctively went up as if she were cradling her child. 'I remember the feel of Kieran,' she whispered. 'The strength in his sturdy little body. The way he hated to lie down, always wanting to be sitting up and looking around inquisitively...He—he hated having his vest pulled over his h-head...'

Her body drooped as tears filled her eyes and emotion clogged her throat. And she decided that she had to leave without delay. But before that, Lorcan must somehow learn the truth. Gritting her teeth in an effort to hold back the tears, she said painfully, 'Harry wanted an heir. He wasn't interested in me as a person. I was a means to an end. I— I want to tell you what we decided together but I can't because I promised faithfully,' she said, wishing she could break her word.

'Let me guess. First he offered you marriage—'

Her eyes flicked up. 'Oh, no, he didn't!'

There was a shocked gasp from Lorcan. 'Not marriage?' he said in amazement.

'Everyone believed we'd been secretly married in London because that's what he told people. But we hadn't.'

Lorcan was breathing heavily. 'You and he were never married!' She could see him running through the consequences of that revelation. 'You have no right to Ballykisteen Manor!'

'None at all,' she confessed. 'And I apologise for deceiving you but I was protecting Con.'

'You're telling me that you agreed to be Harry's mistress,' he said in astonishment, 'and that you *pretended* to be married for convention's sake? How could you do that? Couldn't you see that you were repeating your own mother's role in life—that of sex and housework?'

'I agreed to nothing of the sort!' she said indignantly. 'Only my first husband and you have ever made love to me.'

Lorcan was so angry his body shook. 'That's a lie,' he blazed. 'Babies don't grow on trees. Or did he rape you in a drunken moment?' he shot in a vicious growl.

'He never touched me. And I've never been raped.'

'What do you mean? That doesn't make sense!' he declared.

Suddenly she felt tired, barely able to continue, her whole body listless with misery as the story wound to its conclusion and her departure loomed horribly close.

Lorcan jumped up and restlessly paced the room, concentrating fiercely on unravelling her secret. All of a sudden he stiffened, and she knew he'd hit on the answer.

'Artificial insemination!' he shot like a pistol crack.

'Yes, Lorcan,' she sighed, glad now that the truth was out. 'Con was born through artificial insemination. That was our arrangement. I wanted a child badly. When Harry described how it would be for me to hold my baby in my arms…' She choked back a sob. 'I couldn't resist. The thought of being here, of filling the emptiness in my heart with a baby, was too much for me in my weakness.'

'The swine!' Lorcan muttered.

'Was he? I don't know. He gave me Con. I had a bad time with Harry, but I built up my own business and re-newed my friendships.' She pushed back her tumbling hair with a weary hand, aware that this was the end. 'As you see, Con is Harry's child, but he's technically illegitimate with no claim on the estate at all. I'll pack now. I'll be out of your hair, out of your life—'

'What?' Lorcan felt his whole body contract with pain. 'You can't go!' he found himself blurting out roughly, his fists tightening till the skin over his knuckles showed the bone beneath.

'Don't be idiotic. Of course I have to!' she sobbed.

His brain, his fine, legal brain, had ceased to function. The only thing in his mind was an overwhelming sense of desolation.

'You—you'd be destitute,' he said, grabbing at straws, anything to keep her there. 'Let's calm down and talk sensibly, see if we can work this out—'

'We've tried. I've thought till my head's almost burst! I only know one thing: that I won't be used again!' she flared, her hair flying around her head as she tossed it in furious defiance. Flinging open the dressing room door, she stretched up on tiptoe and removed her clothes, hangers and all, in one impatient movement, throwing them onto the bed. 'No man's ever going to make a convenience of me. I'm going to stand on my own feet, rely on no one and nothing!' she hurled hysterically.

'You can't leave now!' he said in panic. 'Not in the middle of the night. You're not taking Con out in this weather!'

'As if I would!' she scathed. 'But I can leave this room, can't I? I'll collect all my possessions and be gone soon after dawn—'

'Leaving me to cancel the wedding arrangements, to notify everyone?' Another straw, another delaying tactic. Anything, anything, he thought, to hold her in his vision for a few more moments.

'Is that all this is to you? An inconvenience? What do you suggest? I don't want Con involved in any arguments or bad atmospheres. We've postponed this moment for too long. We hurt each other. We're not good for one another and that's a f- fact.'

Appalled now her decision was becoming a reality in his numb brain, Lorcan watched her small, determined figure as she crossly thrust her possessions anyhow into a case. They were both going, she and Con. Her mind was made up. Ballykisteen would be like a morgue without them. And suddenly he felt desperate.

Jamming his hands in his pockets, he felt the ring beneath his right fist and enclosed it in his palm. 'I don't want you to go!' he cried out before he could stop himself.

'No, I bet you don't!' she snapped, abandoning her futile attempt to stuff her teddy bear into the bursting case. His heart lurched at her frustration. 'You'll have to find someone else to satisfy that active libido of yours!'

He reeled at the gibe. She was nursing her teddy, tears bright in her huge eyes. Something tore across his heart. The indigestion had come back, too. And his mouth was dry. He felt physically sick. If she left, he realised with a shocking clarity, his world would fall apart. Kathleen was everything to him. The whole world.

He caught his breath. There was nothing wrong with his

digestion and never had been. This was raw emotion. Pain. There was so much scorn and hate in her eyes that it was hurting him. This was the worst rejection he'd ever known. Kathleen had been the centre of all his plans for the future and now she was exercising her right to walk away from him.

Aghast, he assumed the mask he'd always produced when in danger of exposing his hurt.

'If anyone is to leave,' he said quietly, 'it should be me.'

That stopped her in her tracks. She dropped the teddy bear and gaped. 'You?' she said in astonishment.

To his mind came a picture of her, roaming another town or village, friendless, miserable and homesick, and he knew he couldn't allow that; he cared too much about her welfare. She must be protected at all costs. At any cost.

'This is your home more than it is mine. Your friends are here. You've built up a thriving business and, as you pointed out before,' he said, adopting a cool, reasonable tone, 'there are many people who rely on the work you give them. I can live anywhere, set up office anywhere. My work takes me around the world. Keep Ballykisteen. Because...' He swallowed, overcome by the rogue emotion—and furious that his even-handed delivery had been ruined. 'Because I have...affection for the Manor,' he went on tautly, 'I am more than happy to ensure its upkeep. I'll settle an annual amount—'

'It doesn't make sense,' she said suddenly, looking alert and watchful. 'Why should you walk away from what is rightfully yours?'

His mouth clamped shut as an upsurge of tears threatened to betray him. So he shrugged and turned away. 'I've just explained. I have some decency in me.'

'It seems so...generous,' she said thoughtfully. 'Especially for a man who loathes the sight of me.'

'So I'm generous. Why not?' he muttered, wondering if

that had sounded as hollow and as desolate to her as it had to him.

'Lorcan, face me and say that,' she breathed.

Face her. When he wanted to take her in his arms and kiss her into submission because she mustn't leave, it would break his heart... Furious with himself, he swallowed to ease the terrible closing of his throat.

'Don't make a big deal of this,' he forced out. 'I'll write the initial cheque and—'

To his horror, she was in front of him, peering shrewdly up at his befogged eyes. She stood there, her robe gaping open, her body infinitely desirable in the lace nightdress, which made bewilderingly pretty arcs across her breasts.

He felt his heart somersault uncontrollably and he reached out in blind panic to push her away, but she grasped his arms and stood firm.

'Lorcan. I've been honest with you. It's time you were honest with me,' she whispered.

Why should he reveal his heart? What benefit would there be in telling her how he felt? He loved her with an intensity that scared him. Perhaps he'd felt like that for a long time and he'd just misread the signs because he was too stupid, too darn dumb to recognise the symptoms. But he couldn't tell her now. It was too late and he didn't want her pity.

'There's nothing to say. Don't prolong this,' he clipped.

'So you're going from here, from me,' she said, cruelly prompting a stab of anguish in his aching heart. 'We won't make love again. Never hold hands, walk the Famine Road, sing together, wake in each other's arms—'

'Stop it!' he raged.

'Why? It can't matter to you, can it? I was only a convenience, wasn't I? You'll find another woman to bear your children,' she said callously. 'You don't care that we'll never grow old together, watching the blossom bloom and fall or see the birth of our children—'

'It *does* matter!' he roared, unable to bear the dead, lifeless future ahead of him without the woman he loved. 'I love you, Kathleen! I love every hair on your head, every pore, the curve of your waist, the way you cluck over those goats and chickens, the warmth of your smile, your tender and loving heart…*everything*.'

He caught her arms, determined now to woo her back, to win her…and to hell with the fear of rejection. The stakes were too high to give up.

'I love you so much it *hurts*!' he exploded. 'I love you enough for both of us. I never had any intention of using you. When I said I wanted children it was because I wanted *your* children. Oh, hell, I mean…'

'I know what you mean, Lorcan,' she said softly, her eyes bright with tears. 'I suspected—'

'No, you don't, you can't!' He ploughed on, sure she could never know the full extent of his feelings. 'You are my other half. My soulmate. Without you I'm only half a person. Every cell in my body was put together just for you. I've been so angry with the men who've hurt you because your pain is my pain—'

'You were angry with…them—not me?' she breathed, looking bemused.

'If they'd been on this earth I would have hunted them down and forced them to grovel at your feet,' he said grimly. 'Don't you see? I want to protect you, to care for you and Con and the marmalade cat and the tortoiseshell one, and Scratch and Scruff—'

'Shall we,' she murmured, winding her arms around his neck, 'take your concern for the animals as read? There's an awful lot of them to work our way through and we have other things to do.'

'Like what?' he said guardedly. He hardly dared to hope,

his heart sounding a tattoo in his chest as she smiled be-
guilingly at him.

'Lawyers!' she exclaimed in affectionate amusement.
'What do they know? Do I have to spell it out for you?
You have to kiss me,' she said happily. 'Then you take my
clothes off, then I slowly ease off yours, then we make love
and then you propose to me all over again and I accept.'

'What…are you saying?' he breathed.

'It's simplicity itself. Pay attention,' she purred. 'You
wanted me to stay in the house you have always loved and
you were willing to leave. That means,' she said as if she
were talking to a congenital idiot, 'that you must care a
great deal about my welfare and my feelings. And I was
prepared to surrender the house and area I loved, my business, friends and my own son's future here, because I
couldn't bear to be near you and not to be loved by you.'

All the tension flowed from his knotted muscles as her
words filtered into his brain. She loved him that much, he
marvelled. She'd been through hell and back and now she
was here in his arms.

'I want you to be happy more than anything in the
world,' he said desperately into her soft hair. 'I'll do everything I can to get you to Libya so that you can see
Kieran's grave and you can put him to rest in your mind
and be more at peace with his loss.'

'I'd like that very much,' she said fervently, her sparkling eyes showing that she had been touched by his
thought.

'I love you, Kathleen!' he said in triumph. 'I love you!'
Then he dared to take a greater risk. 'Do you really love
me?'

'With all my heart and soul,' she whispered, reaching up
to kiss his mouth. 'So much that I'm bursting with it.'

He held her close, his eyes brimming with tears of happiness. 'This emotion stuff…'

She laughed and raised a slender eyebrow. 'Yes?'

'It gives you a wonderful feeling, doesn't it?' he said in awe.

'It gets even better,' she promised. And began to show him.

COMING NEXT MONTH

MILLS & BOON®

Presents...™

THE BRIDEGROOM'S DILEMMA *by Lindsay Armstrong*

When Skye admitted she longed to have children, just weeks before their wedding, Nick couldn't hide his doubts. When Skye walked away he was devastated. Now Nick must convince Skye to give their love another chance...

HUSBAND ON TRUST *by Jacqueline Baird*

In the seven weeks since their whirlwind wedding, gorgeous entrepreneur Alex Solomos has transformed Lisa's life. She tells herself she's being foolish for thinking it's all too good to last—until she makes two shocking discoveries...

THE ONE-WEEK BABY *by Hayley Gardner*

When a baby boy was left on West Gallagher's doorstep, Annie was there to help out, and in doing so she fell in love. West, however, had vowed never to have a family. But perhaps looking after little Teddy might help change his mind...

THE TAMING OF TYLER KINCAID *by Sandra Marton*

Who is Tyler Kincaid? And why does he think he can lay claim to Jonas Baron's Texan ranch, Espada—and Jonas's stepdaughter, Caitlin? She wants Tyler—but will he ever reveal the secret quest that has bought him to Espada?

Available from 3rd March 2000

COMING NEXT MONTH

MILLS & BOON®

Presents...™

MILLS & BOON®

Catherine George

introduces the *Dysart family*

continuing the popular Pennington saga.

The family live at Friar's Wood, a grand
nineteenth-century house and own a
well-respected auction house.

Over the coming months, join the next
generation of Dysarts in their quest to find love
and a partner for life.

A Vengeful Reunion - 7th April 2000

Lorenzo's Reward - 7th August 2000

PLUS more from the Dysarts in 2001

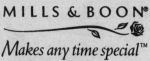

MILLS & BOON®

By Request™

Three bestselling romances brought back to you by popular demand

Latin Lovers

The Heat of Passion by *Lynne Graham*
Carlo vowed to bring Jessica to her knees,
however much she rejected him. But now she
faced a choice: three months in Carlo's bed, or
her father would go to jail.

The Right Choice by *Catherine George*
When Georgia arrived in Italy to teach English
to little Alessa, she was unprepared for her uncle,
the devastating Luca. Could she resist?

Vengeful Seduction by *Cathy Williams*
Lorenzo wanted revenge. Isobel had betrayed
him once—now she had to pay. But the tears
and pain of sacrifice had been price enough.
Now she wanted to win him back.

*Available at branches of WH Smith, Tesco,
Martins, Borders, Easons, Volume One/James Thin
and most good paperback bookshops*

FREE!

4 Books
and a surprise gift!

We would like to take this opportunity to thank you for reading this Mills & Boon® book by offering you the chance to take FOUR more specially selected titles from the Presents...™ series absolutely FREE! We're also making this offer to introduce you to the benefits of the Reader Service™—

- ★ FREE home delivery
- ★ FREE gifts and competitions
- ★ FREE monthly Newsletter
- ★ Books available before they're in the shops
- ★ Exclusive Reader Service discounts

Accepting these FREE books and gift places you under no obligation to buy; you may cancel at any time, even after receiving your free shipment. Simply complete your details below and return the entire page to the address below. *You don't even need a stamp!*

YES! Please send me 4 free Presents...™ books and a surprise gift. I understand that unless you hear from me, I will receive 6 superb new titles every month for just £2.40 each, postage and packing free. I am under no obligation to purchase any books and may cancel my subscription at any time. The free books and gift will be mine to keep in any case.

POEB

Ms/Mrs/Miss/Mr ....Initials...............................

BLOCK CAPITALS PLEASE

Surname..

Address...

....

....Postcode ....

Send this whole page to:
UK: The Reader Service, FREEPOST CN81, Croydon, CR9 3WZ
EIRE: The Reader Service, PO Box 4546, Kilcock, County Kildare (stamp required)